FIRE PRINCE

QURILIXEN LORDS: A QURILIXEN WORLD NOVEL

MICHELLE M. PILLOW

MICHELLEPILLOW.COM

Fire Prince (Qurilixen Lords)

Fire Prince © copyright 2022 by Michelle M. Pillow

First Printing April 26, 2022

Published by The Raven Books LLC

ISBN-13: 978-1-62501-279-1

ABOUT FIRE PRINCE

Charming a dragon prince might be her people's only hope. Too bad the handsome shifter can't be trusted.

From NY Times & USA TODAY Bestselling Author, Michelle M. Pillow, a fantasy science fiction romance!

As an ambassador for the dragon-shifter monarchy, Prince Kane is well aware of his responsibilities. The shifters might have expelled the evil Federation from their planet and freed their alien prisoners, but they're left with chaos and opposing factions threatening civil war.

This is not the time for Kane to be thinking

about romance, especially with Nova, a daredevil leader who rattles his calm and tempts his inner fire. The rousing woman's ideas go against everything he and his people are trying to accomplish.

Before a virus wiped out their home planet and they relocated to Shelter City, Nova's mother had been a revolutionary leader. It's a role Nova has inherited. If outside threats weren't enough, age-old conflicts are fracturing her people during a time they need to band together. Unfortunately, they're isolated and greatly outnumbered, and everything she holds dear is on the line.

Charming a dragon prince might be her people's only hope. Too bad the handsome shifter can't be trusted.

A Qurilixen World Novel

QURILIXEN LORDS SERIES

Dragon Prince
Marked Prince
Feral Prince
Fire Prince
Her Lawless Prince
Poisoned Prince
Cursed Dragon

"Filled with intrigue and adventure, Dragon Prince: A Qurilixen World Novel is an exciting new spinoff in a rich and intricate universe. Michelle Pillow creates characters to cheer for, to hope with, while building worlds that are portals for the imagination. Truly, Ms. Pillow is a master of futuristic fantasy."

Yasmine Galenorn, NY Times, Publishers Weekly, & USA TODAY Bestseller

"Michelle Pillow weaves a fantastical tale of dragon shifters, full of rich world-building, action and adventure, along with a sexy love story. This entire series is not to be missed!"

Bianca D'Arc, USA TODAY Bestseller

AUTHOR UPDATES

Join the Reader Club Mailing List to stay informed about new books, sales, contests and preorders!

http://michellepillow.com/author-updates/

*To my wonderful readers. Thank you for your love
and support all these years.*

SHELTER CITY, PLANET OF QURILIXEN

"This isn't a game. Keep going. Be quiet! We don't want the soldiers to find us." Nova pressed her back against the jagged metal siding of the ration distribution center and kept watch of the alley's only opening. Her legs strained as she lifted on her toes to see over the hunks of rusted debris littering the path.

Her eyes watered from the smoke that hung thick over the city. Above the pungent rolling cloud, dragons dominated the sky, breathing fire in giant blasts to raise temperatures below. Loud explosions sounded, indicating the dragons probably weren't the only ones setting things on fire.

Chaos rang out as people stormed the streets—blindly brandishing rocks and metal poles. Almost any object they could carry had been weaponized.

Her people, the Cysgodians, had known this day would come. And for most, dying in battle would be a badge of honor and preferable to living under the continued tyranny of the Federation. Their numbers were small. Victory would only be possible if they joined forces with the shifters.

Nova lifted her hand for silence as she watched another group charge past. Their entire beings focused on the fight ahead. They didn't glance down the alley to where she hid with Tanja.

"I want to fight," Tanja insisted, breathing heavily as she resumed digging in the red-tinted earth. "They'll call us cowards if we don't."

Tanja had all the bravery and stupidity of a sixteen-year-old raised in Shelter City. Her childhood had been filled with mud-caked rusted metal, near-endless sunlight, and a level of poverty that would shame most civilizations.

"Death is not glamorous," Nova answered. They were hidden between two buildings in a dead-end alley. She didn't want to use Tanja for this task but stealing food rations was about as safe as anything else in the city right now. "Burning in fire even less so."

"Do you like the cats or the dragons more?"

Tanja mused as if being in the middle of a battle didn't frighten her.

"Neither," Nova answered. "They both stood by and watched as the Federation mistreated us for thirty years. Just because they show up now to help doesn't redeem that fact."

Unlike Nova, Tanja had never known another way of life. She'd been born between the two cliff walls of the vast gorge, an alien visitor overseen by a militant organization that used them as pawns to piss off the native shifters. The girl had seen the Federation drag people away, never to be seen again. That kind of upbringing jaded a person.

Tanja struggled with the shovel, breathing heavily as her digs weakened.

"Hand me that." Nova kneeled on the ground and reached for the homemade shovel. Tanja leaned against the side of the building to take a break.

"Dragons are scarier because they can fly away after they breathe fire on us," Tanja continued, ignoring Nova's answer to her question. "But cats are braver because they stay on the ground and fight face-to-face. They can't fly out of reach."

Nova stabbed the ground and pried up dirt. They needed enough space to grab the edge and cut a hole. The metal walls wouldn't have been buried too deep into the ground. "There are plans in place."

"Cats or dragons?" Tanja insisted. "If you had to choose."

"I don't know. Dragons," Nova dismissed. "Now listen to me. There are plans in place in case a day like today happens. I need you to get as many food rations as you can to your best hiding spot. These are only for you and the other young ones. Understand me? You have to take care of the others. They can't fend for themselves."

"Fine." Tanja looked up toward the sky as a dragon cast a shadow over their hiding spot.

"I'm serious. No tributes to any of the factions. No trades for magic potions or vials of shifter blood to give immortality. All of that is nonsense. You tell no one where you hide them." Nova grunted as she slid the shovel's tip along the hard red dirt to loosen it.

"They're saying Doyen killed a shifter in the forest, and that is what started this." Tanja continued to look up. "Do you really think the Blood Fanatics drink shifter blood?"

"He's all talk." Nova dismissed the gossip over the Blood Fanatic leader. "If he killed a shifter, they wouldn't be helping us fight the Federation."

"Unless they do it so they can take control," Tanja countered.

"I'm pretty sure this started over that woman General Sten strung up in the marketplace." Nova stabbed at the dirt. Aside from guesses and rumors, she wasn't sure what had spurred this battle or how the dragon- and cat-shifters had gotten involved.

"That's Justina," Tanja said. "I've listened to her ranting at the marketplace about thieves and secret tech. People say she's crazy, but some of the stuff she says makes sense. Guess the general didn't think she was too funny. I wonder what she said to make him mad enough to punish her."

"We'll probably never know," Nova said. "Whoever ends up taking over won't tell us any more than they have in the past."

"You're talking like we're going to lose." Tanja frowned.

"No matter what happens today, we won't be in charge. In order to win, we need to be in control of ourselves."

Nova stopped digging as she reached the bottom lip of the metal wall. She held out her hand and pointed toward the laser straight cutter. Tanja passed it to her.

"Even if we beat the soldiers today, we'll lose

eventually." Nova wedged the cutter under the siding, hooking it against the metal. "Those dragons and cats outnumber us. You can't trust any of them. They all have motives that do not consider what we want."

"Drone," Tanja warned.

They both froze and waited for the surveillance to fly over them. When it was gone, Nova pulled the cutter upward. The device fizzled, struggling to burn through the metal. Like every other piece of technology in Shelter City, it was old and near useless.

While struggling to force the cutter up through the metal, she continued, "They don't want us here, and they are under no obligation to take care of us. The last thirty years are proof of that. The Federation will not tolerate this rebellion. We might get rid of General Sten, but they'll send more soldiers. The best we can hope for is to escape to a small patch of forest where they can't find us. For that, we need a plan. We need food."

"So you have decided to lead like your mother?" Tanja asked.

Nova didn't know how to answer. She knew what was expected, just as she knew the cost of such a position. For years she could put off officially accepting her inheritance because there was no power to wield. With this rebellion, her hand was being forced.

"Here, let me." Tanja tried to take over. After a small resistance, Nova gave the laser to her.

Nova stood. Soldiers in black uniforms ran past, brandishing their weapons as they charged rebelling Cysgodians. Foot traffic had started to increase. She stepped out a little farther to better hide Tanja from view with her body while keeping watch. Better they detected her than the girl.

Very rarely was she the cause of the things that happened in her life, but Nova had to deal with them nonetheless. She didn't ask for this rebellion, but it was here. When a virus wiped out most of her planet and the decision to move to Qurilixen was made, she wasn't asked what she wanted. There were times she thought it would have been better to die with the others.

Images of the past tried to surface. It had been decades, and still, their sting had not faded.

"You!" A harsh voice barked the word like a command.

Tanja gasped.

Nova jumped in surprise. Her thoughts had just drifted for a moment.

"Get out here," the man ordered.

Nova waved her fingers behind her back, telling the girl to stay hidden. She stepped out to face a soldier. His shaved head was bald but for a small patch of black hair at the crown. Her eyes automatically went to the name on his black uniform. *Mure.*

"If you have a weapon, throw it down." The soldier motioned his blaster pistol at her.

Nova lifted her hands to the side to show she did not.

A second man appeared next to him. "Leave her. The fun is this way."

Nova tried to read the second man's name but couldn't make it out. Cold green eyes glanced in her direction. She knew that dispassionate look well. He and a hundred of his friends had it. They resented being stuck babysitting the Cysgodian people. When those soldiers looked at their alien charges, they didn't see people. They were livestock, to be penned in and contained because the bosses said so.

"We have orders to bring them all," Mure answered.

"Why are you licking the general's ass for a promotion?" Green Eyes tried to pull his friend's arm. "With your family's connections, you'll be out of here in a year and a general within ten."

"Because I know how to obey orders." Mure grinned, and she couldn't tell if he was joking.

"What's she going to do?" Green Eyes chuckled. "Trust me. You don't want anything that diseased whore is offering."

Nova stiffened. That comment took a very dark turn.

Mure almost looked apologetic for his friend. Almost. But the expression seemed somehow rehearsed and didn't meet his eyes.

Green Eyes lifted his blaster pistol as if to shoot her. "Looks like another casualty—"

Nova yelped, curling her body forward as she lifted her hands to block her face.

Mure bumped his friend's arms to redirect his aim. A shot fired overhead. "Not yet."

Green Eyes snorted. "No one will care."

Nova wanted to run but didn't dare move to expose Tanja. The alleyway behind her was a dead end. Her heart hammered violently, and she tried to catch her breath. She willed the girl to be quiet.

"I'll catch up." Mure gestured for his friend to leave.

"It's your trip to the medical booth." Green Eyes didn't hesitate to take off.

Another drone flew overhead, this time stopping

to record the situation. Mure angled his nametag toward the device and then gestured it to fly away. The drone obeyed.

"Get out here," Mure ordered with a wave of his blaster. "Don't force me to shoot you."

Nova heard Tanja making noises behind her and shuffled her feet as she took slow steps forward to mask the girl's sound. She wove her way around the giant metal scraps that had been stored between the buildings.

"I'm not fighting," Nova managed as she tried to catch her breath. Suppressed tears burned their way into her eyes. She didn't want to die. Not today. Not like this. Not raped and murdered in an alleyway.

Stay quiet. Stay quiet. Nova willed Tanja to heed her thoughts.

The roar of fire sounded, followed by pistol blasts and clanks of metal. Screams rose in the distance. It became impossible for her mind to separate the present from the past.

She'd been old enough to remember the bodies of the sick lining Cysgod's streets, the darkness of death contrasting the shiny city buildings. There had been too many, too fast. Some of the people had been put out too soon. Nova used to have nightmares about those poor moaning souls trapped in their diseased bodies.

Fear further jumbled her thoughts as flashbacks from the past overlayed the present.

The Cysgodians had burned the deceased, choking the air. Her brother had morbidly called it the smell of a thousand corpses.

Now, here, dragon fire lit up the Qurilixen sky in long bursts. Burning canvas flapped along the side of a building.

Then, the Cysgod government workers had shot the dying where they lay in the street before moving on to prevent the less sick from future misery.

Now, Federation soldiers shot in battle to subdue the rebellion. The *pop, whiz, pop* of the weapons was unmistakable.

Then Cysgodians had fought to defend themselves.

Now they fought to attack.

Everyone screamed. Both past and present echoed inside her in a symphony of pain and terror.

Nova tried to calm her breathing, but her eyes focused on the tip of Mure's blaster. In one fatal second, every decision could be made for her. She wouldn't have to choose to lead the Revolutionists faction.

As if not perceiving her as a threat, Mure lowered his weapon. "Walk that—"

Nova didn't think. She balled her hand and swung, taking Mure by surprise. Her fist slammed into the side of his face. His head knocked back and clanged against metal scrap before he fell to the ground.

Nova stood over the man in shock over what she'd done. When he didn't move, she looked around to see if anyone had seen her. Thankfully, there were no drones.

Tanja appeared from behind. "That was—"

"We have to hide him," Nova interrupted. She ignored the pain in her hand as she grabbed Mure's leg. Tanja joined her, and together they dragged him into the alley.

"What if he wakes up? We should shoot him." Tanja ran to pick up the blaster pistol.

Nova blocked the man. "No. We're not like them. We don't do that."

"He was going to take you," Tanja said, determined. "I've seen them do it. I know the taking look."

Nova's heart sank into her stomach. "Tanja, have the soldiers taken you?"

"I'm too fast," Tanja denied. "Not everyone is fast."

"Was it reported?" Nova kept between Tanja and Mure.

Tanja looked at her like she was daft for even suggesting it. Who would they tell? Who could do anything?

"Was it this guy?" Nova pointed back at Mure.

"They all look the same," Tanja said. "They come from the shadows in their uniforms. In the daylight, it's easier to spot them, but when the dark night comes..."

The girl referred to the one night a year that the three suns set at the same time, casting the valley into darkness. The rest of the time, varying degrees of soft green light illuminated everything. On Cysgod, they'd had many nights of darkness, but to those born on Qurilixen, they weren't used to the dark and had developed their own scary myths around the night. Seeing Tanja's expression, she knew maybe all their stories weren't myths.

Nova wanted to tell the girl that it was all right. That this was not how life was supposed to be. That there was something better waiting for them, some-where else, in the future, so close.

Hope. She wanted to give her hope.

A dragon swooped through the streets, large wings flapping so hard a blast of air hit Tanja from behind. It caused the girl to stumble forward.

A blast shot from the pistol.

Pain burned through Nova's thigh, and she cried out as she fell to the ground. She caught herself on Mure's face and instantly drew her hand away when she felt wet warmth. The blast had passed through her leg and into Mure's skull.

"I didn't mean..." Tanja dropped the pistol. Someone ran by the alley's opening, and they both stiffened. The person didn't stop.

"With your family's connections, you'll be out of here in a year and a general within ten," Green Eyes had said.

Blasted stars, who was this soldier? What connections?

"This never happened," Nova stated, panicking as she looked at the sky. She found it clear of drones. "You were never here. No one has seen you."

Tanja didn't move as she stared at Mure's body.

"Tanja, say it," Nova ordered.

"I was never here. I didn't do it. No one sees me," Tanja whispered. All the girl's bravado from earlier faded under the reality of the death she'd caused. Killing a Federation soldier was not like murdering someone from the city. Sad, but completely accurate.

"Good girl. Now get out of here." Nova put pressure on her leg.

"What about the...?" Tanja gestured weakly toward where they had been trying to break into the ration distribution center.

"You were never here," Nova repeated, grunting as she put pressure on her leg in a poor attempt to stop the pain. "You were hidden when that drone came by. No one knows you were here."

Nova hoped that was true.

"But..." The girl gestured at Nova's leg. Tears rolled down her cheeks.

"Find a place to hide. Stay away from the fighting. Run fast." Nova slipped her hands down her bloody thigh to stop the bleeding.

Tanja took off down the street.

Nova struggled to stand and limped her way toward the blaster pistol. She couldn't leave it out in the open. There was no telling who would find it.

Everything was wrong. This is not what was supposed to happen. They'd had a plan.

If a rebellion broke out, they would need to focus on food, medicine, and shelter, regardless of who won. If the Federation won, they would punish them for the uprising, which could include starvation. If the shifters won, they had no obligation to help. If the Cysgodians won...

Nova gave a small laugh as she limped away from the alley carrying the pistol. The last thought was a child's tale. Cysgodians never won.

2

SHELTER CITY HAD FALLEN.

Now the real work began.

Kane landed on the cliffside watchtower, talons gripping the circular roof as his wings rose and fell with heavy breaths. Trails of smoke filtered into the air, the remnants of a long-overdue fight. Battles were ugly affairs, and the view left a bitterness in his throat. For decades he had spent sleepless nights trying to reason a diplomatic end to Federation occupation. This was not an answer he would have come up with.

In his dragon form, his eyesight was enhanced, and he could see the sprawl of the alien city in perfect detail, even from the great height over the valley. For thirty years, the city of decay and rust had stained the once beautiful region. Pieces of jagged metal pierced the ground bearing sun-worn canvas like dirty flags of capitulation. Together they formed what could be called housing if the definition of the word bore no resemblance to civilization.

Kane focused on the flow of Cysgodian people celebrating in the streets. He hoped they enjoyed the moment and embraced it. There was no telling how long it would last. When the smoke cleared and the dust settled, uncertainty would replace the tyrannical rule.

What now?

The question lingered in his mind. As an ambassador for the dragon-shifters, they would come to him for answers to that question. This situation had been discussed. The shifters had plans in place. Whether the Cysgodians went along with the plans was another matter. Contact between the shifters and the alien refugees had been limited, blocked by the Federation.

Shelter City was always meant to be temporary, a place for the alien visitors to recover from a virus that had wiped out most of their homeworld. The Federation had brought the Cysgodians and their plight to Qurilixen's doorstep and laid the responsibility of saving them at the feet of the shifter royals.

General Sten knew full and well that honor would bind the shifters and force them to help. King Ualan of the Draig dragon-shifters and King Kirill of the Var cat-shifters could not say no to saving hundreds of lives. To the shifters, denying the Cysgodians healing sanctuary was as bad as killing the aliens themselves.

The Cysgodians would think this moment meant freedom. But what would that look like?

Factions in the city hated shifters, some even wanted them dead in a flawed notion that drinking shifter blood would make them immortals.

Fools.

Shifters would think this meant liberation from the Federation's occupation. Kane knew better. The Federation wanted a base on their planet, and they would not give that up easily. Today, they drove out General Sten, but others would come in his place.

Maybe we are all fools.

His people had never wanted to be part of the Federation Military's Alliance, but the Federation used the Cysgodian tragedy and their illness to gain a foothold on the planet. They claimed squatters' rights because they had dominion over the makeshift city, and the shifters refused to agree that city was anything more than a temporary settlement—to do so would be to accept the alliance. The result had been this occupied graveyard of rusted ship parts and crumbling stones.

On the other side of the valley, structures of a different nature sat above the city of corrosion and rot. The evenly spaced buildings ran along the ridge of the opposite cliffside. Unlike the structures below, those buildings weathered the constant daylight of the planet, looking as if they had just been constructed.

Lording above it all stood a stone monstrosity, a single rectangular structure with metal arches along the rooftop that sprawled over the entire length of the city. He hated the building. There was no natural beauty to the industrial lines. The shifters took pride in how their planet looked. His palace home blended with the beauty of the mountains.

Kane could just make out the figures in front of the eyesore as his cousins and Var royals escorted General Sten off their homeworld. Today was a good day in that regard. Most of the cats and dragons were in half-shift, walking upright like men but protected by the shell of their animals. Several soldiers were being loaded into temporary holding cells.

The Cysgodians had been the real victims in the

political standoff. They had no power, no home-world to return to, and no choices. They had been trapped within the valley's borders, between two cliffs—one with a dragon watchtower and the other monstrosity where General Sten and his top advisors lived...well, or *had* lived until today.

For decades, shifters had been trying to free Shelter City from the tyranny of the Federation. And this was the exact moment they'd finally succeeded.

At least, for now.

Kane heard his brother flying before he saw him approach. Wing flaps were much like footsteps. Live with someone long enough, and those sounds were as telling as a voice. Pyke hovered above him, looking out over the city for a long moment. Brown wings tipped with black created a unique pattern on his brother's shifted skin. Kane was happy to see him uninjured. Not all dragons had been so lucky.

With that thought, he concentrated on the flow of the city, focusing on people who were not moving. Once he looked for them, they were easy to pick out from the chaos. The black uniforms of the fallen Federation soldiers separated the enemy from the allies.

He found a woman rocking on the ground as she

held someone. Her cries couldn't be distinguished from the roar of celebration. The death toll could have been much worse, but that news would not bring comfort to the woman. Several men carried bodies, moving to line them up on a shaded walkway while others cleared piles of rubble.

Drones flew through the sky. Moments before, they had blasted warnings from the Federation. Now they broadcasted Var Queen Lyssa's voice as it repeated a message, "We have food. We have medical. We have decontaminators. Please stay in the city. Everyone will be helped. We have food. We have medical..."

Pyke twisted in the air and dove for the watchtower window beneath where Kane perched on the roof. The momentum of flight carried his brother's body forward as he shifted midair and entered the tower window. Kane leaned his head over the side to watch him land safely. Seconds later, Pyke poked his head out and shouted, "We're to head down to help with the wounded. Here, take clothes."

Pyke tossed up one of the tunics they kept stored in the watchtowers, followed by a pair of pants. Kane caught them in a taloned fist. Their Aunt Olena had devised the stashes to help with the fact that all of Kane's generation lost their clothing when fully shifted. The older generations did not turn into full dragons, and they kept their clothing when in man-dragon form. Not everyone appreciated naked shifters running around the countryside.

Pyke dove from the watchtower in his human form, gripping several pairs of clothing in his fists. His body shifted as he fell toward the ground. About a foot from hitting, he flapped his wings and righted his trajectory toward the sky. He coasted from the cliff, the clothes fluttering like banners as he dove into the valley below.

Kane watched his brother briefly before turning his attention back to the city.

A lone woman limped along an abandoned street. He tracked behind her to where a fallen soldier lay.

Kane watched where his brother landed. The other shifters had gathered on the other side of the valley. The wounded woman wasn't near medical help. When he again searched for her, she'd stopped walking and merely stood.

Kane's wings settled, and he didn't move as he observed her. Something kept him from flying off his perch. He felt the warmth of fire building in his throat. The involuntary sensation took him by surprise as he did not need to protect himself or send a signal. Still, fire erupted long and loud from his throat.

Kane knew his family would be looking at him in question, wondering why he sought their attention. He automatically signaled with his wing to show all was well. Let them think he celebrated.

The woman had also turned to watch him. Her black hair twisted at the nape of her neck, leaving only a few tendrils to frame her face. They blew in the soft breeze, and she made no move to push them from her blue eyes.

Those beautiful eyes searched the distance, unable to see him as clearly as he looked at her. He felt the fire burning its way back into his throat as if to show off the natural skill. He suppressed it, and instead a tiny puff of smoke filtered out of his nostrils. Why was the dragon part of him trying to show dominance over the city?

Or was it trying to do something else?

Kane's eyes focused on the woman. She remained, just standing and watching him as he watched her. For the longest moment, they stood transfixed. The rest of the city faded into the peripheral. He became aware of the pressure of the wind against his hardened flesh. As a dragon, he didn't feel the coldness of it.

What was she doing?

Who was she?

His eyes remained focused, his vision tunneled as if they could divine the answer for him.

The woman swayed slightly at first. Soon, her body rocked back and forth with greater movement before collapsing altogether.

Kane instantly surged from the tower, diving into the city to get to her. She didn't pick herself up from the ground as she lay motionless on her back. His heart beat hard in his desperation to check on her. Why hadn't he flown down sooner?

He landed on the dirt street with a heavy thud. His talons gripped the clothes his brother had given him, dragging them a few steps as he walked toward the woman. He released them, leaving them on the ground.

Her eyes rounded in fright at his approach. She had markings at her temples that were a Cysgodian genetic trait. Hers happened to be blue like her eyes. She rolled onto her stomach and began to crawl away from him. Her fingers dug into the dirt, and her leg dragged behind her. Suddenly, she stopped and reached for her waistband. She struggled for a moment before turning onto her back. Dirt caked a bloody wound on her thigh.

Kane halted as she pointed a blaster pistol at him. A blast would sting, but it wouldn't injure his dragon skin.

The woman's mouth opened, but she didn't speak. Her chest heaved for breath.

Kane forced his body to shift. His bones cracked into place, and the hard shell of his dragon form softened into the skin of a man. Now a blast could kill him, but he didn't think she wanted to harm him.

He lifted his hand and stepped forward. "I'm here to help."

The gun dipped, and her lids fluttered over her eyes before both dropped as she passed out.

Kane rushed to her side to check her. She breathed, not quite as heavy as before. The edges of her wound looked singed even as it seeped blood. She'd been shot.

Kane ran to grab the clothing and tore the tunic shirt. He wrapped the material around her leg and knotted it tight to stop the bleeding.

The pistol caught his attention, and he turned to look in the direction she'd come. Though he couldn't make out the soldier completely, he saw enough of the man's injured head to know he was dead.

People died during battles and uprisings. It was the cost of war and ending tyranny. This situation became complicated because of the Federation. It could be assumed that General Sten wasn't forthcoming when reporting back to his superiors. They were going to want answers for every soldier's death. It would be best for the woman if they couldn't prove what she had done.

Kane let his dragon overtake him once more. Fully shifted, he tossed the weapon into the air and blasted it with fire. By the time it fell to the ground, it was a melted hunk of metal. He flicked it with the tip of his tail and sent it flying toward the cliffside forest.

The woman hadn't moved. He took hold of her arms and lifted her gently from the ground to carry her to where they could give her medical attention.

3

NOVA STOOD ON THE CLIFF BESIDE THE DRAGON watchtower overlooking Shelter City. In the weeks since the battle, not much had changed on the surface. Rusted metal still jutted from the ground. Old canvas flapped in the breeze.

What *had* changed couldn't be readily seen. It was a feeling. Hope, yes, but mostly fear. The Federation had been a known dictator. Its abuses and tactics were somewhat predictable after thirty years. Now her people faced the unknown.

Shifters.

For thirty years, the shifters had stood by and watched the decay, and now they wanted to help?

Nova didn't trust them. None of the Cysgodians did. Well, except for Justina, who'd gotten the shifters to acknowledge her as a leader. The woman had no Cysgodian authority to lead, but the shifters didn't seem to care.

The shifters had offered them medical care and food. They said pretty things and made promises. Nova was old enough to remember the medical care, food, and false assurances the Federation had given them. There was no reason to believe the shifters would be any different.

Time would reveal.

A feeling of exhaustion came over her. She walked to the edge of the cliffside. Until recently, she hadn't seen this view of her home. The height caused her heart to beat a little faster. She wondered what it would be like to leap from the edge and fly away.

Away.

The word whispered through her. It was a dream she didn't let herself have often. To be able to leave, to go away. Such freedom. Such luxury.

Such nonsense.

Nova felt her mother's invisible hand pressing down on her shoulder. The memory of it was so ingrained that the sensation kept her grounded. She had a responsibility to her people. She didn't want the role, but she had inherited it.

People looked to Nova to lead them like they had her mother before her. If the unknown threat of shifters wasn't enough, old factions were starting to emerge as if no time had passed. Before the virus, Cysgod had been in the midst of a revolution. They liked to wax poetic about shiny buildings and clean living, but the truth was age-old conflicts had fractured their society long before they came to Shelter City.

Each faction wanted to be the one to speak for the Cysgodian people, and they all had differing ideas on what that meant. The dragons had agreed to meet with all of them. If Nova accepted the invitation, she would cement her role as a leader. Her life would not be her own.

It already wasn't.

Nova inched closer to the edge, watching the tips of her worn shoes jut over the side.

Away.

One would think they could get themselves together long enough to join—

"Don't."

Nova inhaled sharply in surprise at the sound. The shock caused her to lose her balance, and she tipped forward. Flailing, she tried to find hold in the air. She screamed in terror as she began to fall.

A strong force grabbed hold of her shirt and jerked her back from the edge.

"Don't."

Arms wrapped around her. The contact caused her to stiffen. She wasn't used to being held.

"Don't," the man repeated, his gravelly voice not readily familiar.

Hardened brown skin revealed he was a dragon-shifter. The strong arms clamped her like a vise, too powerful to pry away. Nova dropped her shoulder and struggled to be free. To her surprise, he let her go.

"Don't jump."

Nova turned slowly, almost scared to face him. Her heart pounded from her near fall. "Then don't startle me."

She wished the words were more forceful.

As she finally looked at him, it was to find the hard-armored flesh molding into his more pliable human form. An eye ridge disappeared into his fore-head. Not so pliable were the muscles of his naked chest. He wore a loose pair of pants and nothing else. Since the rebellion, it wasn't unusual to see the shifters running around naked after they trans-formed—not all, but a good many.

She stared at his face. Short brown hair blew

around his head, and whiskers stubbled his jaw. Perhaps even more stunning than witnessing a transformation was the starkness of his green eyes. They seemed to glow from within, demanding she meet his gaze. She had seen those eyes in her dreams, only they hadn't been in a handsome face.

"You weren't going to jump?" The man sounded relieved.

Nova frowned. "Not exactly the *away* I was looking for."

"So you have decided to go on the ships?" he inquired. "I had not realized they'd already made the offer. You are up here to say goodbye to the city?"

Nova's frown deepened. And here it was. The unknown.

"You're transporting us off-world?" Nova took a deep breath and held it. Where would her people go? The planet of Cysgod was uninhabitable for at least another hundred years.

"Those who wish to go," he answered. "You're not our prisoners."

Nova couldn't help but smirk at that. She kept her eyes on him while nodding in the direction of the city below. "We're not? What would you call it?"

"Guests," he stated, and he actually seemed to believe it.

After a moment, she realized she agreed with his assessment...somewhat. Guests. Not neighbors. Not friends. An obligation.

"And our welcome is over," she concluded. "Where are you sending us?"

"Anywhere you wish." He stepped closer, and she kept her eyes steadily on him.

"I wish to go thirty-five years into the past," she answered.

At that, he sighed. His lips pressed together. After a long moment, he said, "You must look to the future. If you don't wish to leave, there will be other options presented by your leader."

"Our leader?"

"Lady Justina."

Nova couldn't suppress her laugh. So much for faction leaders being given a chance. "Justina? So that rumor is true? You're setting up Justina to be our supreme leader? The woman who stands on the street corner covered in mud, screaming conspiracy theories? She makes us all look insane. Who put her in charge? Was she standing in the right spot, and the shifter royals just pointed at her and said, 'Sure, why not? You're all idiots anyway. You can speak for them.'"

"She is the reason you are all free," the dragon-man stated.

"Sleeping with royals has its perks," Nova muttered in response. Everyone knew Justina had attached herself to a cat-shifter prince. The couple had made no secret of it.

"She risked her life bringing evidence of—" The man held up his hand. "It's not my place to say more."

"No, say." Nova crossed her arms over her chest. "Present the options to me."

"There are protocols," he said by way of an answer. The man began looking around the ground. He shook his hand back and forth to encompass the area. "Have you seen a leather band? I lost a bracelet."

"Protocols?" she prompted.

"It has a stone on it," he continued.

"No. I haven't seen it," she stated. Before repeating, "Protocols?"

"Yes, protocols. The official way things are meant to be handled." He gave one last look around and frowned as he rubbed his naked wrist. "I must have lost it during the battle."

"Can you make a new one?" she asked.

"It's...never mind." He turned his steady gaze to her once more. "May I escort you back down?"

She shook her head. "I don't think I'll get lost."

"I need to..." He pointed at the sky. "Wait, I meant to ask. Your leg?"

"My leg?" Nova touched her thigh where she'd been shot.

"Are you...? Is it...?"

"Better, thank you. I haven't noticed any radiation sickness from the medical lasers they used." Nova stared at his face, trying to place if she'd seen him before. How did he know about her leg? It wasn't the worst wound to come out of that day. "Someone named Nadja fixed it for me."

"Yes." He smiled and nodded. "That's my mother."

Nova realized that must have been how he knew her. He'd probably been around the medical tent, and she'd been too out of it to notice. "She was kind to me."

"She is kind," he stated.

Nova glanced over the city. The heads of the factions would be gathering soon. Some of them anyway. "I should go."

He nodded, watching her. It was impossible to

tell what he was thinking by the expression on his face. "Don't..."

"I'm not jumping," she answered.

"Don't give up hope in the future." The man ran past her toward the cliff and leaped.

Nova ran to the edge to watch as his falling body transformed. His pants ripped from his legs and fluttered down. Wings shot from his back as his body distended into its dragon shape. He dipped before darting past where she stood. He went up into the sky. Within seconds, he was halfway across the valley heading toward the Federation's old stronghold.

4

Kane landed on the other side of the valley near the stronghold facility. Part of him wanted to fly back to finish the conversation. Or at least attempt an actual conversation in which he sounded intelligent. Instead of "don't," he could have formed a sentence. Maybe, "please, be careful on the cliff." Instead of, "my mom is nice," he could say, "my mother is a trained scientist who saves lives and who has formulated medicines for our people."

Or he could *not* talk about his mother to the pretty woman.

Perhaps he needed more rest. The weeks since the rebellion had been filled with meetings and strategic planning. The Var royals had been to the

Draig palace, and in return, the dragon princes had been to the Var palace.

And now they were all going to meet with Cysgodian faction leaders to try and keep the peace as they figured everything out.

In all his years as an ambassador, that conversation with the Cysgodian woman was Kane's lamest attempt at making a diplomatic impression. For some reason, seeing her again caused his words to come out in twisted, unintelligible half-sentences. When he looked at her, his thoughts had flown all over the place.

Sacred dragons. What was wrong with him? He shouldn't be worried about talking to women at all. Or out looking for his damned mating crystal, even though his father kept reminding him he needed to find the bracelet.

Kane shifted from his dragon form and stood naked overlooking the city. He glanced at his bare wrist. To his shame, he didn't know the moment he'd lost it.

The stone had been given to him when he was born and had stayed with him throughout his life. A dragon's crystal represented the most important thing to his people—love. There were theories on how it worked, everything from magic to metaphysical energies, but the truth was it worked. The crystal would glow when a dragon-shifter met the person they were meant to spend eternity with, indicating what biology already knew. Since dragons mated for life, it represented their one chance.

Why was he thinking of this now?

Why were his eyes straining to see the other side of the valley where the woman stood? The woman whose name he didn't know. The woman who had lingered in his thoughts since he'd rescued her. The woman with eyes of clear blue and black windblown hair.

He should have asked her name.

He should have given his.

He should be focusing on today's meeting.

"That's an interesting offer, but I'm going to have to pass. Our elders would read too much into it, and then Korbin and Grace won't be the only arranged marriage in the families."

Kane frowned at the playful voice and turned his attention to the cat-shifter princess, Payton. They'd known each other since childhood.

She nodded toward his hips and laughed. "That's one way to greet the city."

Kane realized his manhood was completely erect and quickly drew his hands to hide it.

"Modesty?" She arched a brow. "That's a new dragon trait."

"I wasn't thinking about..." He glanced over the city.

Her. He kept thinking about her.

"Not me?" Payton laughed. The princess might seem delicate and fragile, but he'd seen the form of a white tiger rip from her body. He'd fight beside her any day. "You must be worried. I've never seen you this distracted."

Kane glanced around for a stash of clothes.

As if sensing his search, Payton pointed to the nearby trees. "Over there. I was tempted to steal them and make you all walk around naked at the meeting. Then I figured today was not the day for pranks, and I think everyone has seen enough of you naked guys running around."

"I heard they're working on a new material that will stretch and change shapes. Perhaps the next generation will be able to shift with clothing on." Kane went to where pants, tunic shirts, and boots were stacked into neat piles on a tarp. He quickly dressed.

Seeing three sets of clothing left, he knew some of his cousins had yet to arrive. The older generations of dragons, aside from their late grandmother

Queen Mede, didn't shift into full flying dragon form and did not need stashes of clothes. Cat-shifters solved the full-shift clothing issue by wearing clothes with cross-laces along the sides. Their clothing fell off their cat bodies, and they could retrieve it later.

Not all of the cousins would be joining the meeting. Some would be overseeing the overhaul of the barracks.

"Is everyone here?" Kane asked as he pulled on his boots.

"Roderic and Justina are for sure. They just went inside. We were in the forest talking to those marsh farmers."

"Marsh farmers?" Kane prompted.

"The lion brothers." Payton nudged one of the unclaimed boots with her toe, forcing it to lift and thump a couple of times on the ground. "They inter-cepted us in the forest and demanded a royal audi-ence. They're the perfect example of what generations of drinking and feral living will do to a bloodline. I hate to wish loneliness on anyone, but the gods might be doing us a favor if that brood doesn't procreate."

Kane stood, fully dressed. "That can't be good if the marsh farmers are willingly trying to talk to you.

Are Cysgodians leaving the city and going into their territory?"

Payton shook her head. "Curtis and Fergal are worried because Valter is missing. They're convinced he's dead. We think he's probably dead drunk. It wouldn't be the first time they lost the location of one of their moonshine stills."

"Were they here for the battle?" Kane eyed the trees in the direction of the Var palace as if he could somehow cut through the distance to see the answer. The lion brothers had kidnapped his cousin's wife when she'd first arrived on the planet and had wanted to turn her into the Federation for a reward. Nothing good came from that family of cat-shifters.

"They would never." Payton shook her head in denial. "Honestly, I think the whole thing was a waste of time. Curtis especially is a shifter purist. He's not happy about today's negotiations and probably wanted to put a stop to them by making up a story. He would never help non-shifters. He'd trade with them at most, but the lion brothers don't believe in intermingling with aliens."

"Ignorance," Kane muttered.

"Something isn't right with you. What is it?" Payton touched his arm. "Has there been news about the Federation?"

Kane shook his head in denial. "No. Tori and my mother have not received an answer through the mediators. Pyke and some of the cousins have been dispatched into space to await the inevitable arrival of the Federation ships. Until then, we wait."

"I don't know how you ambassadors do it. I hate going through intermediaries. I doubt they'll adequately express our displeasure over this whole affair." She sliced her hand through the air to make a point. "I want to confront the situation straight on and speak for ourselves. Or, in this case, punch them all in their smug faces."

Kane understood the impulse and kept his voice calm. "And that is why you are not an ambassador."

"Yeah. For the best." Payton chuckled. Even though she smiled and kept her tone light, he saw the worry in her eyes. She took this as seriously as the rest of them but buried her feelings under the careless attitude.

"We do it this way because we know it is best to let the ESC act as a moderator. They will be able to back our scientific investigations. It is the entire reason we were justified in expelling General Sten from the planet."

The Exploratory Science Commission had sent scientists to test a drug General Sten had been distributing to the Cysgodians under the guise of vitamin supplements. It turned them hostile, increasing fighting in the city. Over time, it would have turned them murderous.

"We should have pushed General Sten off the side of the cliff," Payton muttered.

"They would have sent someone to replace him and used it as an excuse to mark us as hostile and take over the entire planet. In the long run, this is the best for our people." Kane took a deep breath.

"Ah, but you have to admit, watching him fall and splat would have been satisfying." Payton looked out over the city. "I suppose these are our people too. No one would take them when they were sick, and the Federation offered incentives. I can't imagine any planet is going to take them like this. I can't help but wonder what would happen to them if they left. They needed the radiation from the blue sun to fight the virus, and the disease is most likely dormant in them. What's stopping it from mutating and coming back if they leave?"

"The scientists need more time before we can answer that." Kane made a move for the door. "I must go in."

"I'll go with you," Payton said.

"The Var sent you to this?" Kane asked in surprise.

Payton shrugged. "All cat royals are pitching in."

Kane nodded. Who was he to question the Var's decision to send Payton? He led the way toward the stronghold facility. There were no Federation soldiers left to block their entry. He placed his hand over the wall scanner, prompting the doors to open.

Stepping inside, they were greeted by two Var guards. The men were half-shifted into the forms of upright cats—half-man, half-animal. One gave a low growl to Payton, and she frowned at him.

"You brought it on yourself, Natan," Payton told the man with a dismissing wave.

Kane didn't bother to ask about the interaction.

The white, pristine walls had an oppressive quality to them as they walked down the long corridor. The doors were evenly spaced on either side. There was no art to their creation, no real craftmanship. It figured the Federation would create such a place. They thrived on utilitarian function and had little regard for aesthetics. These places were prefabricated in some alien warehouse and shipped out for easy installation.

"This facility is an eyesore," Payton said. "Yevgen asked if he could have it. I think he was only half-joking. I want to give him access to the database. He can analyze it faster than our people."

"You mean your husband?" Kane teased. "Are you angling to make this your cyborg palace?"

"Uh, you too with the jokes?" Payton scrunched up her face in annoyance.

"Grier told me Yevgen was asking a lot of questions about cat-shifter half-mating. You could do worse than a cyborg hacker who's averse to sunlight on a planet cast in constant daylight," Kane continued. His cousin and future dragon king, Grier, had dealt with Yevgen on many occasions. The cyborg lived in Shelter City, crammed into a small alcove between buildings as he monitored everything while hiding from Federation detection.

"Good ol' Commander of the Var Guard would love that," Payton mumbled. Prince Falke was easily the scariest of the Var shifters and Payton's overprotective father. Unfortunately for familial bliss, Payton had a wild streak that could not be tamed. The two were locked in a battle of the wills that started the second Payton learned how to shift.

"Will Prince Falke be joining us today?" Kane asked.

"He is busy deploying troops to strategic locations around the planet with my brother, Hunt, in case there is a Federation attack. My mother is coordinating with Ryland in space, trying to get him home. However, I think part of her wishes it was the other way around. I think she misses her space pirate days."

The sound of voices came from ahead. As if on cue, they both stopped walking. They tilted their heads to listen.

"Why are we here? What do they have to offer us that we can't take for ourselves?" a man whispered. "I'm tired of being told what to do. It was bad enough when it was the Federation, but now we're under the rule of these alien animal creatures? Their actions have proven they do not want us here."

Kane shared a look with Payton. They remained still. The voices came from around a corner.

"Hold your tongue, Doyen. They'll hear you," a woman scolded.

"He has a right to express his concerns," a second man inserted.

"Concerns?" the woman scoffed. "I don't want his rhetoric speaking for all of us."

"Let's agree. No one speaks," the second man insisted. "Let's hear what they have to say, and convene—"

"I will speak for my followers as I deem necessary," Doyen dismissed. "Shifters don't frighten me."

"This doesn't have to be like the old ways," the woman insisted. "The fighting did us little good on Cysgod before the end. The factions can come together for a common purpose. If we join forces, we're united and stronger. There aren't many of us left."

"Agreed. Anytime your Peacekeepers want to pick yourselves out of the dirt and join us, Efa, we'll enthusiastically start your initiation," Doyen said, the words followed by a light thud.

Doyen gave a menacing laugh. A woman stumbled into view as if pushed.

Efa had a slight red discoloration at her temples that matched her darker red hair. Rounded eyes found them as the woman realized Kane and Payton had overheard. She quickly straightened her shoulders and hurried back the way she'd come. Footsteps could be heard rushing down a corridor.

"Don't know about you, but I have a good feeling about this meeting," Payton drawled sarcastically. "I've seen recordings of Doyen's speeches. I had hoped he would not be here. That man should not be allowed to speak. I still for the life of me don't understand how he's alive. After we stopped the still from exploding, Jaxx and I were sure he was dead. We were in a hurry, but still... I mean, we buried him in an alleyway."

"Just don't admit that to anyone else. It will only give his mythology credence." Kane gave a rueful shake of his head. "I don't want him here either, but we can't dictate whom the factions have chosen to represent them. Better to see him for ourselves and judge. Rhetoric about blood can't be used as proof without an actual crime to tie to it. If it were, we'd have to arrest every bad storyteller."

"He tells people that drinking shifter blood will give them a long life," she said. "That's more than a bad story."

"Still not a crime. We still must sit down with him. Perhaps we can reason with him."

"Did I remember to tell you I hate diplomatic duty?" Payton straightened her shoulders as if to stiffen her resolve.

"Yes, I believe it was mentioned."

They fell into step, turning into the corridor from where the voices had come.

Kane had been in the facility many times over the years, and they easily navigated their way through a series of turns. Every hall looked the same

—more white walls, ceilings, floors, and endless lines of doors. Boring. Ugly.

"We should decorate this place with a nice big bonfire," Payton suggested, clearly thinking of the building's unattractiveness as well.

The sound of running footsteps came from behind. Grier appeared. His face was flushed as he pulled a tunic over his head. "Are we late?"

"Plenty of time," Kane said.

Grier gave a sheepish grin. "The wife needed me."

"Is Salena well?" Kane asked. Salena had a unique natural ability. She could draw the truth out of anyone simply by asking...and sometimes not asking. "Did she learn something?"

Grier's grin widened, and he chuckled.

Payton nudged Kane in the side. "Stop asking. We don't want details from the marriage bed. Mated couples always overshare to those without mates. It's like they can't help but brag."

"Oh, no," Kane amended. "Don't answer that. No, you are not late. We were just going in."

"You really are distracted today," Payton observed yet again. "Maybe you should get some sleep after this."

Kane wished that were possible. After this, he

needed to fly back to the Draig palace and make a report, so dispatches could be sent to the dragons living in the north, away from the drama of the borderlands.

"I heard about your crystal." Grier patted Kane's shoulder.

Kane glanced at Grier's wrist. His cousin used to have a crystal sewn onto his bracelet, but since he married and no longer needed a mating crystal, he'd replaced it with a broken piece of blue pottery.

"I'm sorry," Grier continued. "We're all keeping an eye out for the stone. We'll find it."

Kane's father had apparently sent out an alert to the family when his son didn't find his crystal fast enough. The man had been eager for a daughter-by-marriage ever since his nephews, Grier and Jaxx, had found their mates.

Kane's desire to find love could not be a priority right now.

He thought of the woman he'd left on the cliff.

Payton glanced at Kane's wrist. Her smile fell. "You lost your mating crystal? I'm sorry. I know how much those mean to you."

Cat-shifters did not have such devices when it came to mating and love, which was quite honestly why they always seemed to have a rough go of it, and even ended up with several half-mates. He would never say the judgment out loud, but it made little sense to him.

Kane gave a little nod to acknowledge their concern before pushing through a set of doors. Inside, the conference room matched the annoying white walls and floors of the rest of the complex. The lingering smell of disinfectant lasers fragranced the air.

A white table gleamed with a glossy finish, reflecting the three Cysgodians who had been speaking in the hall moments before. Efa did not meet their gazes. He wondered which of the two men was Doyen. Neither looked at them.

"Welcome," Kane stated, ever the diplomat. "I am Prince Kane of the Draig. This is Prince Grier. Princess Payton."

The three didn't readily answer as they continued to stand and stare.

"And you?" Kane asked.

Efa looked expectantly at the men before saying, "Efa. Doyen. Jare."

Doyen's gaze lifted and held steady. Anger boiled behind his eyes, appearing to simmer beneath the surface. Kane tried not to judge the man for it, but it was difficult. Rage served no purpose. He made a mental note not to trigger the man's temper lest the talks ended before they began.

Kane gestured toward the narrow chairs placed around the table. The three hesitated and glanced at each other before they sat down.

Jare was the oldest of them if the thin white hair and weathered face were any indications. The man had an underlying tiredness to him as if he had seen many things and did not hold out much hope one way or the other. He reminded Kane of elders in their six-hundredth year. Though Cysgodians did not naturally live to be six hundred, and this man was probably more around eighty—just a few more years older than Kane.

The thought of mortality circled in his mind, contrasting their differences. Kane appeared as he had fifty years ago.

Being reminded of the fragility of life firmed his resolve to find a solution. These people had come to Qurilixen for help because a virus overtook their homeworld, and they were forced to relocate or die. They'd already lost too much.

Kane heard footsteps long before King Ualan and King Kirill joined them. The royals had been on opposite sides of a war in their youths, but time had calmed any animosity between them. In some ways, working toward the common goal of helping the Cysgodian people had helped many of the elders see beyond past hurts.

With them, cat-shifter Roderic escorted his mate, Lady Justina. Like Kane, Roderic's father was an ambassador, and it made sense that he attended. Justina had been placed in a position of authority over Shelter City because of her role in its liberation. She was someone they could trust.

Ualan smiled at Grier and touched his son's arm. "Your mother wishes to see you at dinner tonight."

Grier nodded.

"What is she doing here?" Doyen asked, his voice much louder than the others. "She does not represent a recognized organization."

"We recognize Lady Justina," Roderic stated, defending his wife.

"Dirty whores screaming in front of the marketplace are not considered a faction," Doyen stated coldly. His gaze dared Roderic to react. The cat-shifter stiffened, and claws sprouted from his fingertips.

Kirill lifted his hand, stopping Roderic from responding. "All will be discussed in due course after all parties are present."

Doyen grinned, the look mocking. Efa appeared as if she agreed with his assessment of Justina but not his handling of it. Jare stared at his reflection on the table.

Not surprisingly, the shifters had a mountain of bad feelings and suspicions to climb. The Federation had lied to Cysgodians for so long that many of those lies were accepted as truth.

Kane saw the anger in his friend and knew Roderic struggled to keep his shifter side buried. Doyen was a fool. One slash of Roderic's hand and the Cysgodian faction leader would bleed out on the floor. Justina touched her husband's arm and whispered in his ear. Whatever she said instantly calmed him, and he nodded.

"I believe we're waiting on Tork?" Ualan observed, gesturing to the shifters that they should be seated.

"We'll be waiting a long time. He died from his wounds yesterday," Jare answered.

"Wounds?" Kane took a seat across from the man. "What wounds?"

"From the battle," Jare stated.

Kane shared a look with his uncle. Ualan gave a small shake of his head, confirming he didn't know.

"I do not remember his name on the wounded list," Kane said.

"Not all of the wounded wanted to be on your list," Doyen answered. "Or exposed to more radiation poison."

"The medical lasers that the shifters use are safe." Justina came to the table. "I've had them myself. The shifters are not like the Federation."

Justina stopped talking when Doyen openly scoffed at her argument. Kane could see the rumors about the man being a problem were not exaggerated.

"We are sorry for your loss." Kane knew they couldn't make the Cysgodians trust them, at least not right away.

Payton and Grier sat to his sides. Justina kept away from the others, choosing to be near the end next to her husband. The kings remained standing.

"Are there any organizations, groups or factions unaccounted for?" Ualan asked the group.

"None that matter." Doyen noticeably liked the sound of his own voice. He couldn't seem to help himself.

"Possibly," Justina answered. "Shopkeepers?"

"Wouldn't they be a guild? How is work a faction?" Payton whispered to Kane.

"In the time before," Jare answered softly, his eyes lifting to Payton, "Cysgod had three hundred and sixty-seven known factions. Most did not survive because the members and their interests died on the planet. Today, eight are left."

"So we are waiting for five more," Ualan concluded.

"Three at most," Efa said, folding her hands in her lap. "Tork will not be replaced. The old medical faction has yet to choose a leader or their course. There are the Childbearers who take an interest in the children. And, as Justina said, Gethin for the marketplace. And have the others confirmed a leader yet?"

No one answered her.

One of the Var guards appeared in the doorway, still half-shifted into a man-cat. "The transport arrives."

"Thank you," Kirill dismissed with a nod. "That should be the rest of our guests."

"I thought this was a meeting of equals," Doyen responded. "What makes us your guests?"

"Be reasonable," Efa said under her breath with a frown. "They own the planet. *Guests* is the appropriate term."

"This is our home," Doyen countered, "as much as theirs."

"No," Jare disagreed. "This is not our home. Our home is dead."

Grier nudged Kane on the leg. Kane shared a knowing look with his cousin. They would make sure Jare received help for his moods if he needed it. It wasn't uncommon for the older generations to keep past tragedies in their heads and become overwhelmed by sadness.

Again footsteps proceeded the remaining members. King Kirill walked out of the doors and waited in the corridor. "Please, join us. We have yet to begin."

A tall, thin man entered. Orange markings on his temples said he was Cysgodian, but he also had a translucence to his skin that was not normally seen on Qurilixen. Red irises appeared to be of natural coloring.

"Gethin," the man stated as he went to a seat next to Efa. "I represent the Shopkeepers in the marketplace."

"Of course they're in the marketplace," Doyen said.

"Lowri." A woman entered, her gown pieced together but clean. Her hair was brushed neatly into a bun as if she took great pride in her appearance. "I represent the Childbearers."

Kane leaned toward Grier but forgot what he was going to say when he heard, "I'm Nova. I represent the interests of the Revolutionists."

His head whipped around to the woman in the doorway. At the movement, her steady blue eyes met his. Surprise registered for a brief moment.

Nova. Her name. Nova.

Beautiful Nova.

Kane's heartbeat quickened, and he pressed his hand to the table, automatically wanting to stand and greet her. He began to smile, only to stop as she moved her eyes from him as if they had never spoken. Her gaze stopped on Doyen. The man smirked. Nova gave a slight shake of her head as if warning him to keep quiet. To Kane's surprise, the man said nothing.

Kane lowered his hands beneath the table and remained seated. Efa, Jare, and Doyen reintroduced themselves before the shifters did the same.

When it was his turn, Kane glanced at Nova. She pointedly did not look at him. "Prince Kane of the Draig, royal ambassador."

The woman stiffened slightly, her head tilting away from him. The gesture was subtle.

Kane wanted to speak to her, but now was not the time. And Nova didn't exactly act like she wished to talk to him.

Kirill closed the doors. The others finished with introductions, and the kings took their seats.

"We understand that you might mistrust our intentions," King Ualan began the meeting. They had carefully prepared all they wished to discuss.

Doyen audibly smirked. Nova shot him a stern look, and he schooled his expression.

Kane watched the interplay carefully. Who exactly was this woman?

5

THERE WAS NO TURNING BACK.

Nova's heart hammered in her chest even as she endeavored to remain calm. The pressure in her throat made it difficult to breathe. She had seen Kane fly toward the facility, but she hadn't expected him to be in the meeting or a prince. For some reason, she'd assumed messenger or guard. Any positive thoughts she had toward the man had to be pushed aside. They were on opposite sides, and their intentions would not align—how could it be any other way? He represented the shifters' interests. She had a responsibility first to her people. She spoke for those who could not or did not know how to deal with politics.

Claiming her role as a leader was everything her

mother had ever wanted for Nova. She'd spoken endlessly about it in her last years, making her daughter promise to accept the birthright. Like many of her people, her mother had clung to the old world and had not been able to let it go. When other children played fun games, Nova had been made to practice handling various diplomatic situations. At the time, it had seemed pointless living in a one-room home with a dirt floor.

"We understand that you might mistrust our intentions," King Ualan stated.

Nova tried to remain calm as the weight of responsibility burdened her shoulders. She looked at her fellow faction leaders, knowing that they distrusted her as much as she did some of them. So many people looked to her for guidance. She couldn't botch this up.

"But," Ualan continued, "it is our intention to lay out the facts as we have them. First, all indications are that the virus has been rendered dormant. More tests are needed to confirm that the radiation from the blue sun has eradicated it. Future mutations are always a possibility, but currently, there is no threat to your population. With immunity, it's possible that any mutation will be naturally dealt with. Our scientists are setting up testing labs inside this facility."

Nova couldn't form words, so she sat quietly staring at the king's face. She knew she should look away but was unable to do so. These were pretty sentiments, but her mother had taught her to be suspicious of everyone's motives.

"Your living here, in that regard, can be looked at as a success," Kane added. "You came here to be cured and, for the most part, that has happened."

Nova glanced at him and quickly away. She couldn't look into his eyes for too long. He made her thoughts swim in her head, and she needed to focus.

"Testing labs? We will not be experimented on." Lowri started to stand. Nova placed her hand over the woman's, stopping her. Lowri looked like she wanted to protest but finally settled back into her seat. She crossed her arms over her chest.

"You might be late to the table, but no one has died from the virus for decades. The Federation kept their word on that," Efa stated. "They had more experience with this sickness than you have with the aid of our medical research. While I appreciate your scientists taking an interest, we know what we need to do to stay healthy. The current precautions have kept us safe."

"Kept their word?" Doyen snorted.

"They said they'd stop the virus, and they did." Efa frowned and refused to look at Doyen. "We have more pressing problems. What is happening with acquiring food rations? The distribution centers are nearly empty."

"Perhaps tell them about the food simulators," Justina prompted.

"We know the hardship the Federation ration program put on your people." Kirill leaned forward, threading his fingers and placing his hands on the table. "As the last of the soldiers are escorted off the planet today, we will continue to install food simulators and will teach your distribution center workers how to use them so they can teach others. There will be no more rations."

The shifters watched them as if they expected a celebration.

Lowri smiled and started to lift her hand.

"To kill us faster with dangerous radiation?" Doyen answered before Lowri could.

Lowri remained quiet and rethreaded her arms over her chest.

"The simulators are safe. I've tasted the—" Justina began.

"Of course, you would say that. You married a

shifter," Jare interrupted. "I'm sorry, Justina, but your opinion in this matter does not hold weight. We all know what we've seen."

"Everyone should have a chance to speak, Jare," Efa put forth. "Even her."

"I've tasted the food and I'm healthy," Justina finished her sentence, still confident even after being rebuffed.

"The Cysgodians who have eaten the food smuggled in from the simulators have suffered greatly—cramping, lack of energy, vomiting, even dancing in the streets." Jare shook his head. "We will keep to the rations."

"Dancing?" Roderic asked.

"Shaking sickness," Justina clarified.

"Ah, seizures," Roderic told the other shifters.

"We have reason to believe the rations come from food simulators." Justina kept her voice annoyingly calm, as if speaking to children. "We have found no manifests for food deliveries from off-world suppliers, and the Federation was not trading the shifters for a local food source."

"Mere speculation. Maybe records were destroyed as unimportant. The Shopkeepers should control rations," Gethin contended. "We already have the means to distribute. People know to come to us."

"Jare is right," Efa said. "We have seen things. Food simulators are not the answer."

"We would like to examine anyone with this illness," Grier said. "Medical booths are available for full-body scans."

"Introducing food too quickly after not eating can cause health concerns," Kane added.

"This is a perfect segue to medical care," Ualan said. "We know it's been lacking—"

"More radiation," Doyen muttered.

"Please let them speak," Payton sighed, clearly losing her patience with the Cysgodians.

"Doyen," Nova reprimanded, "we should hear everything."

Ualan nodded his thanks. "We intend to give everyone continued access to medical facilities. Until your people can be properly trained to run the machines, volunteers will be available."

"We're not subjecting our children to those things," Lowri denied. "That is where we went wrong before. Dependency on technology isn't an answer. It's a curse, and we will be punished for it."

Lowri seemed to forget she'd been momentarily excited about food simulators. The woman had the personality of a leaf on the breeze. It blew wherever everyone else was going.

Nova focused on her breathing and keeping her expression unreadable. This was going to be a long day.

"What about you, Nova?" Kane's tone was soft, and he looked as if he thought she would somehow agree with them. "What do you think?"

Nova had no choice but to acknowledge him. Handsome eyes tried to gaze into hers, but she resisted their pull. "I think it is in the shifters' best interest to be rid of us. Without us, you have no conflict. Things could go back to the way they were before we came."

Kane's expression fell.

"Hear, hear!" Doyen pounded his fist on the table and laughed. "Finally, someone who speaks reason."

When he'd quieted enough for her to continue, Nova said, "I don't trust everything the Federation has told us, but I also don't trust you. No one has our best interests in mind except us. So we have to go with what we have seen—our facts, not yours. We have seen what happens to those who ate from the food simulators. Eventually, they became sick, as already described. Or, worse, they began to show signs of aggression, and their personalities changed."

"That wasn't the food," Justina insisted.

Nova still wasn't sure what qualified the street-corner rambler to be at the meeting, aside from marrying into the position. None of the Cysgodians had voted Justina into power. She didn't represent a faction.

"We have no proof of that, only your assurances. The Federation invited us to the stronghold and presented their research. Volunteers from the city became ill." Nova's breathing came easier the more she spoke. She'd spent a lifetime training for moments like this. "As for the medical devices, we've used them only out of necessity, myself included, though I had no choice as I was not awake at the time to protest."

"It saved your life." Kane's brow furrowed in challenge. "You would have died."

"So you say." Nova preferred his censure to his kindness. It made it easier to oppose him. "We do not know the long-term effects of medical treatments. Those booths did nothing for the virus. For some, their treatments made it worse. Can they even detect the Cysgod virus? Or did no one care because it was contained to our planet? Our scientists have not had a chance to look at any new data. We cannot agree to the booths at this time."

Payton fidgeted in her seat, her patience clearly all but gone.

"I don't mean this to be rude, but do you have medical scientists?" Grier asked. "It was our understanding most of them remained behind, many the first to get sick. There have been several advancements in the last thirty years, but by all means, send them forward and we will show them everything."

Nova stiffened. They were correct. There were no more scientists left.

"Show me," Nova said.

"What about information uploads?" Ualan asked. "That technology has been around since my youth. Perhaps we can use them to train scientists, and then they can see for themselves. It would take some time to arrange, but we are willing to investigate the possibility."

"Just not that bridal company you used," Kirill said. "My queen can attest that their uploads were less than stellar. I'll have her contact the HIA. They'll have the newest versions."

"You're not uploading any information into my brain with ancient technology," Doyen refused.

Nova knew for a fact the man had always been

contrary. If the dragons had said not to use uploads, Doyen would have insisted upon it.

"Perhaps we stick to the more immediate needs," Kirill suggested. "Clothing is being delivered—"

"Look," Payton interjected, standing from her seat. The chair made an ugly noise as it was pushed back by the sudden motion. "Let's lay it out on the table. The Federation starved you, poisoned you to make you aggressive, and withheld medical treatment and food simulators by convincing you they were bad. It was about control. Not your health. They wanted you scared. They wanted you here. They didn't care about you. They wanted to use you to force us to join their treaty. Now, you're here, and you're not happy. I get that. But we didn't force you to choose the Federation for help. The ESC or the HIA or possibly even the MAPH—*even though they're arguably a bunch of space pirates*—would have gladly stepped in had you called them. We would have helped if you came to us directly."

"Payton," Kirill warned.

Payton hesitated before taking a deep breath. She added in a calmer tone, "I'm only trying to point out what we all know. If not for the Federation, this city would never have existed—"

"So you admit that your goal is to be rid of us," Doyen interjected.

"*Existed*," Payton resumed, "in its current state. Your treaty with them tied our hands. We have had to stand by for thirty years, unable to do anything without risking our shifter populations had we interfered. Then the second my cousin, Roderic," she pointed at Justina's husband, "brought us actual proof of what the Federation was doing, we all came here and stopped it. We're still stopping it."

"Payton," Kirill warned again, also standing. "Enough."

"No. I'm sorry, my king. They need to know what we have risked and the lives at stake. Thousands of shifters. My family. My friends—some of whom live in Shelter City. The Federation will return to this planet, and they'll want answers. And if they're not happy with what they're presented, we don't stand a chance against their endless arsenal of spaceships. They'll blow us out of the sky and erase us into the deep black. Or overrun us to mine our *galaxa-promethium*. That's all they want. They are a giant, hungry monster and—"

"I said enough. Remove yourself." Kirill sternly pointed to the doors. "Go back to the palace. I will speak to you later."

Payton still appeared ready to argue but finally nodded. She strode from the meeting room, mumbling, "I'm not wrong."

"Clearly passions are running high." Kirill retook his seat. "We all have a lot at stake."

"Regardless of Princess Payton's colorful delivery, she is not mistaken in her general opinion," Kane said. "We will get further working together. If you want to live on this planet—"

"Is that a threat?" Doyen goaded. "Obey, or we kick you into space?"

"An offer," Kane clarified, maintaining his self-control.

Nova found herself staring at the shifter prince, not wanting to be impressed by him. They were literally on opposite sides of the table when it came to the fate of Shelter City. The shifters wanted to dictate and control, but the Cysgodians weren't children to be controlled. They should be able to chart their own course.

Her mother's lessons echoed in her mind. She needed to find leverage, any leverage, to get that control for her people. Blackmail and threats were never pleasant, but sometimes bluffing was all they had.

"This is not how we intended this first meeting

to go." Kane's gaze seemed determined to keep her looking at him.

"You are not our prisoners," Kirill said. "You are our guests. Those who wish to leave the planet will be given access to transportation. We will do all we can to help, but ultimately it is your life to live out in the universes, and we will not dictate it. Those who wish to remain here in the valley are welcome to do so. The barracks will be emptied within a few days and cleaned. Assistance will be given, and rooms assigned to families according to need and size to prevent arguments."

Doyen muttered, but his words were indecipherable.

Kane kept Nova's gaze and continued to focus on her as he spoke. "It is our belief that to make progress we must first start with the basic needs—food, shelter, clothing, and medical checkups. We are prepared to provide all of that. Starting today."

"And if we don't wish to live in the barracks?" Lowri asked.

"You're welcome to remain in the valley. Building supplies will take time to acquire," Ualan said. "Once basic needs are met, our engineers can begin assessing the best way to rebuild."

"And if we don't want to remain in the valley?" Doyen asked.

Kane stiffened. The gesture was small, but Nova saw it.

"It would be best if people remained in the city," Justina said.

"Best, but not mandatory?" Doyen pressed.

Kirill frowned at the persistence. "As leaders, we are all looking for the best possible outcome for everyone. It would not be wise to venture into shifter territories. There are several different views of the situation, and it will take time to settle any misgivings."

At least that felt honest, the king admitting that all shifters were not on board with this plan.

"So yes," Kirill continued, "if we must. Confinement to the valley will be mandatory for the foreseeable future. Assimilation can happen with time."

"Assimilation?" Lowri pursed her lips. "As in forcing us into your ways? Encouraging our children to act like animals?"

Nova grimaced, wishing the woman would stop speaking. Tension rolled through the room as thinly veiled insults and disapproving looks hovered between them.

"The shifters have proven themselves to be civilized," Justina defended. "More so than us at times."

"Not all of us can be bought with a fancy dress and pretty words," Lowri dismissed. "Some of us have values that we don't wish to sell for the price of a wedding garment. We will not be coerced."

"There are many paths. Finding mates among the shifters is just one of them." For the first time since the meeting began, King Ualan's expression darkened. They'd offended him. "Only those matches predestined by the gods will be pursued. No one will be forced to marry. Shifters will never take brides by force."

"Or husbands," Kirill added.

"And what if someone is *predestined* who doesn't wish to be?" Lowri insisted. "Who decides that?"

"The gods." Grier's expression matched that of the dragon king.

Lowri snorted at the answer. "Those are not our gods."

"For dragons, we are shown our mates with the use of a special crystal. The method has never been wrong, and the pairings have proven to be fate." Kane again looked at her as he spoke. The other faction leaders were beginning to take notice of his attention. "However, if a woman or man does not wish to honor the will of the gods as shown, then no one will force it to happen."

Nova got the impression there was more to dragon mating than he was explaining. She couldn't help but wonder how a shifter-Cysgod paring would work. Of course, in human form they looked like ordinary men. There had been enough naked ones running around as of late to prove that. But what about shifted? Dragons in flight did not look equipped for sexual relations, but what about the dragons who walked upright like armored men in clothing? Or the half-man, half-cats that had stood guard when they walked into the facility? She had heard the upright animals refer to it as a half-shift.

"For cats, the process of mating is less straight-forward, but essentially, it is never by force." Roderic touched his wife's cheek briefly and smiled. "Wives are to be honored."

Lowri made a noise of disgust and muttered, "Crystals and mating. Nonsense."

Nova wondered if she could ask Justina about her relationship but quickly dismissed the notion. They were not friends and would not be taking each other into confidence. Nova forced her wandering thoughts back to the situation at hand.

She took a deep breath. This meeting was not as productive as she had hoped, but then she might have been a little naïve, knowing the other faction leaders and their agendas.

Doyen wanted power from chaos and only cared for himself. He got off on trying to control others and manipulation. Sadly, his followers did not see it. Or if they did, they didn't care.

Jare and the few who joined him were simple referred to as Elders. They wanted things to go back to the way they had been in their youth. An impossible ask that, when unrealized, caused them to wallow in pity. They mostly talked about the time before.

Efa and her Peacekeepers pretended to be neutral, and maybe on Cysgod they had been, but life on Qurilixen had hardened them beneath the no-conflict, love-everyone surface. Nova had witnessed more than one of them conflicting with their neighbors.

Lowri and her Childbearers were filled with a kind of elitist hate brought over from their home-world. On Cysgod, they had been rich and power-ful, celebrities. A little mud could not take away that entitlement.

Gethin and the Shopkeepers he represented

would only care about one thing. Profits. With money came control and comforts. Those who controlled the goods had power. Predictably, they wanted to oversee food rations.

Then there was herself.

What did she want for her people? Long life. Happiness. Freedom. Hope. Independence. All those things sounded pretty, but reality was harsh and could easily crush pretty things.

Nova stood and took a deep breath. "As the leader of the Revolutionists, I will accept shelter for my group in the barracks or in the valley. Each person will choose for themselves. I ask that food rations be offered in place of the food simulators. We will not submit to mandatory medical checkups. We thank you for the clothing."

Kane nodded at her decree. The others might have too, but she found herself again focusing only on him.

"Our homeworld is uninhabitable," Nova continued. "We do not choose to go to space. If the blue radiation from the sun has stopped the progression of the virus, we do not wish to lose that antidote."

She felt all eyes focused on her, and she finally

turned her attention to those seated at the table and met each and every shifter's gaze.

"I have heard your thoughts on our coming here. Princess Payton was very clear." Nova stepped around her chair and pushed it toward the table to indicate she had no intention of resuming the discussion. She had heard enough of their plans to know her mind.

"Princess Payton should not have expressed herself so bluntly," King Kirill said.

"But that is not to say you disagree with her. You say we chose the Federation, and that is our fault. I watched my father die through a plate of glass, blood streaming from his face. I witnessed the bodies of my friends and neighbors lining the street. I saw a world die. You cannot imagine what that is like. In your worst nightmares, you cannot know how that feels. You cannot imagine the choices that had to be made. They were not easily done. We didn't just pick the Federation off a communications list. They were the closest. They had a ship large enough to take the survivors."

"We do not wish to diminish your loss," Kane assured her.

Nova gave him a small nod to acknowledge his

words, but it didn't stop her from repeating, "You say we chose the Federation."

She paused, looking at the other faction leaders. For once they did not interrupt. A tear slipped down Efa's cheek.

"You say we chose the Federation," Nova resumed, fighting the pain that tried to surface. "I say in return, you chose to let the Federation come. You could have turned us away. You chose to share this planet with us. We are grateful. But we are also here. This is our home. On behalf of the Revolutionists, we accept your help with the understanding that we will become self-sufficient and leaders of our own territory." She glanced at Justina. "We will choose our leaders, not have them assigned. There will be no mandatory confinement to the valley. We demand the same freedom of movement your people enjoy. It is time we are recognized as full Qurilixian citizens."

"All this can be discussed in time," King Ualan said.

Time. Promises.

The time for promises had passed. Never would they be in such a position of transition again. She remembered her mother's lessons. Revolutionary ideas weren't about being pleasant and liked. They were about forcing change when those in power would resist. The Cysgodians did not have much leverage. However, there was one thing the shifters feared. And it was the one thing she could use to their advantage.

No matter how distasteful she found it.

The life of a leader was not about her comfort.

"If you want our cooperation in keeping the Federation off this planet, you will do more than discuss what I have said. The Revolutionists will do as I say." Nova really hoped that statement was true, but bluff or not, she feigned confidence. "Maybe you found proof of Federation wrongdoing and helped to save us. Maybe we supported Federation rule and knew what they were doing, and you attacked against our wishes. Same event, different views. We'll see which story is told. You know what we want. We have the words you need."

The shifter nobles were shocked into silence. She saw the disbelief on their faces.

Before they could dispute her declaration, she strode out of the doors.

Nova's heart pounded violently, and she tried to inhale deeply without making too much of a sound. Nausea rose in her throat. When she came to the meeting, it was not her intention to threaten the shifters with an altered version of the truth.

A tiny voice in her head that sounded suspiciously like her mother whispered in her thoughts, *Do we know for a fact it was a lie? We have not seen the evidence that sparked the rebellion. We were not asked about it beforehand. You can't trust the shifters any more than you can trust the Federation.*

It felt like poor justification for blackmail.

It was also precisely what her mother would have done.

Nova strode through the halls, wanting out of the corridors. She felt as if the white ceilings pressed down on her.

If she were honest with herself, she'd lost her temper. That was why she'd stormed out. They spoke about the Cysgodians like a problem to be solved, pieces of livestock to be moved from one pen to another. And hearing them lay the blame on her people for choosing to survive, it had been too much.

Nova dashed a tear from her cheek as she hurried past the cat-shifter guards. Though their curious eyes watched her, they did not attempt to stop her from leaving.

6

KANE WATCHED THE FACTION LEADERS LEAVE, feeling as if it had been the most unsuccessful meeting of his career as a diplomat. Not much had been said after Nova's decrees. Doyen supported the threats with an almost sickening glee. Efa, Jare, and Lowri kept quiet. Gethin renewed his bid for control of the food.

When they were alone, Grier let loose a loud moan of frustration. "I don't think that went well."

"You should not have agreed to let Payton come," Kirill said to Kane. "That girl has always run a little wild."

"I didn't invite her. She was waiting for me when I landed." Kane eyed the cat-shifter king. "I assumed you invited her to take a seat at the table."

Roderic tried to suppress a chuckle and failed. He lifted his hand. "My apologies for laughing, but it is no surprise she invited herself. Payton is...*Payton*. She cares about this city and our people. Of course she came. She's Falke's daughter and has a Roane grandmother. She might not have the Roane premonitions, but like her father, she has inherited the burden of their naturally strong opinions. My cousin was born to argue."

Kane stared at the doors. He had the urge to follow Nova to try to reason with her. Payton would not have meant her blunt truth to be an insult, but the result was the same. Diplomacy took finesse, especially when pride and emotions were on the line. Things needed to be prepared and presented carefully. The wrong gesture in some alien cultures could start a war. One visitor he'd dealt with would consider blinking too much a marriage proposal.

"Do you think Nova was posturing, or will she follow through with her threat?" Ualan asked.

The question went unanswered.

"Kane," Ualan insisted. "Nova? What do you think?"

Realizing they waited for his opinion, he cleared his throat and said, "Oh, uh, I don't know."

"But you know her, even though you both pretended otherwise," Kirill stated.

Kane wondered at their pointed looks. "She was wounded in the rebellion, and I brought her to the medical tent. She'd been unconscious at the time. I have only spoken to her once since then, before this meeting."

"Are you sure?" Kirill insisted.

"Kane would not lie," Ualan defended. "He knows his duty."

"I'm not questioning his integrity. Only..." Kirill gestured his hand to the side.

"It did kind of look like more was going on between you," Grier said. "You two couldn't take your eyes off each other. I'm not sure if it was attraction or animosity, but half the time she spoke at you, not us."

"Maybe because she met me before. My face was the most familiar," Kane tried to dismiss.

"I did sense some heat," Ualan noted.

"Why don't you fetch your crystal? See if she can make it glow. Mate her and solve all our problems," Roderic joked.

Justina lightly hit his arm. "Don't send him after the ill-tempered woman."

"She's not ill-tempered," Kane found himself

defending Nova. "She's scared for her people. She only wants what's best for them, and she's using the only tools at her disposal. We can't blame her for that. Our goal should be to establish trust."

"Assessments?" Kirill prompted.

"The middle three will prove to be a minor annoyance but will negotiate." Grier sighed and shook his head as if caught in his own thoughts. "Doyen may be a problem if backed into a corner and forced to prove himself to his followers. Or it might all be bravado. We've known about him for a long time. Yevgen has those recordings of Doyen giving ugly speeches about drinking blood. It could be all talk or the rantings of a lunatic. There is no proof that any of them have actually tried to murder a dragon. Anything from the cats?"

Roderic shook his head. "Nothing on the Var side either."

"Nova should be considered a threat until it's proven otherwise." Grier gave Kane an apologetic look. "I sensed something in her, deep. If she hadn't threatened us, I would have been impressed by it."

"Justina? What do you think?" Roderic prompted. "You know your people best."

"I disagree with Prince Grier about Doyen. Yes, if backed into a corner, the man will fight, but he'll also jump out of the shadows and stab you from behind. His faction has the nickname of Blood Fanatics. We all try to avoid them." Justina looked to where Doyen had been seated. "I believe they'd drink blood if they could manage to take down a shifter."

"Not to brag, but I don't think that will happen," Grier said. "Even the drunken marsh farmers defending their stills would outmatch a Cysgodian attack. With the Federation leaving, everyone is on high alert."

Justina looked as if she might disagree but held back.

"And Nova?" Kane wanted to know about the woman even while regretting the need to ask.

"I was surprised to see her. I didn't know she'd accepted her inheritance." Justina rubbed her temple and closed her eyes briefly as if fighting a headache. "I have mixed feelings on speaking out against her. I know shifters do not mean to harm us. I trust you. I know it in my heart. But I see her point, and I feel her pain. Less than one percent of Cysgod's population survived that virus. Imagine ninety-nine percent of the people you know just gone."

Roderic wrapped his arms around his wife and kissed her temple.

Justina brushed a tear off her cheek and leaned her head back to look at Roderic. "Nova's mother led the Revolutionists on Cysgod. She came very close to overthrowing the government. If not for the virus, she may have succeeded. The woman had a vision of what our society should be."

When she didn't continue, Kane prompted, "Which was?"

Justina pulled from her husband's embrace. "I was young, but I remember reading my parents' newspaper chips. My father supported some of her ideas. She wanted us to reject the alien technologies coming on. She said it shifted our society and made us dependent. Dependence equaled compliance and compromise. Self-reliance was the true path to freedom."

Kane could respect the view. They did not wish for outside governance of their planet, thus the resistance to joining the Federation Military's Alliance.

"But Cysgod prided itself on education and technological advances. Our entire economy was tied to them." She rubbed the back of her neck and struggled with her memories. "If Nova is like her mother, then it would make sense that she distrusts food simulators and medical equipment. It's true that some of the early attempts at a cure that included medical booths were a disaster. Some of the Revolutionists might refuse to use the decontaminators for bathing. It might be difficult to convince them."

"But not impossible." Kane again had the urge to go after Nova. Maybe if he talked to her alone, he could convince her.

Justina dropped her hand to her side. "It will not be in Nova's nature to accept outside help. The only hope I have is her agreement to take the clothes and shelter offered, but that may have been out of necessity. I think we need to take her as a serious threat until, like Grier said, we can prove otherwise."

They considered her words for a long moment.

"Son." Ualan approached Grier and placed his hands on his shoulders. "I am sorry, but we need your wife. I wouldn't ask to exploit her gifts if it wasn't completely necessary. I know how uncomfortable pulling the truth from people can be for her. From the little bit she shared about her dying world, it sounds like Nova carries some horrifying truths. Salena may need to pry them out of her."

Grier hesitated. Salena had spent most of her life trying to block people's truths. Whenever someone went near her, all their secrets tumbled out. Every dark deed and horrible thought. Secrets could be dangerous when people don't want them told.

"Please, Grier. We need Salena to talk to Nova," Kirill added. "We must know if she'll go through with her threats. We cannot take chances with the Federation. They could arrive at any moment. The situation with them must be handled diplomatically."

"We had hoped today would have gone better, and we wouldn't have to ask." Ualan squeezed his son's shoulder before patting it and letting go.

Grier reluctantly nodded. "I'll ask, but I know the answer. She'll do it. She'll do anything to help. She already offered. As has Fiora, should you need both sisters."

Fiora's skill was the opposite of her sister's. Unlike Salena, Fiora couldn't lie when asked a question or even when not asked. The truth assaulted her with visions and spilled out of her mouth.

"Fiora has agreed to help Olek." Ualan looked at Kane. "She and Jaxx are at the palace trying to predict what will happen when the Federation arrives."

Olek, Kane's father, had his hands full at the

palace. He remained near the communications tower as they monitored space.

"What about the other factions?" Kane asked, not liking how they'd singled out Nova, even if she had been the most vocal. "Should Salena speak to them as well?"

No one responded. That in itself was his answer.

"And if my wife discovers that Nova will carry through with her threats?" Grier asked the kings.

"Then we must do everything in our power to make sure that doesn't happen. Every life on this planet is at stake." Ualan appeared almost apologetic. "Kane, keep an eye on Nova until we're ready for the interrogation. It's clear to all of us that there is something between the two of you, whatever that may be. When Salena arrives, you should be here to hear the truth for yourself. We trust you to make the right choice."

Kane nodded. How could he refuse? Especially when the order gave him the one thing he wanted most—to follow after her.

KANE LOOKED OUT OVER THE CITY, TRYING TO
sense where Nova had gone. Two cat-shifters
carried crates from a landcraft into the facility
behind him. He heard their feet shuffling and the
wooden containers thudding as they landed on the
floor. The supplies would be stored until after
everyone was settled in the barracks below.

He moved out of the clearing toward the
surrounding forest to hide from their view. Here,
along the borderlands between cat and dragon territories, the tree bark had a blistered texture as if it
had been scarred by the constant daylight of three
suns. More than once in his youth, they had fash-
ioned clothing out of the large leaves, able to wrap a
single one around their bodies. The smell of nature,

of warm leaves and darker earth, always stirred memories. He could not count how many times they had run through the ancient forest, around trunks big enough to build houses inside, through dense brush and open clearings. As children, they had probably covered every inch of the woods.

He could not imagine losing this world. Or his people.

Roderic's teasing about fetching his crystal had struck a chord. The idea lingered in Kane's mind. What would it mean to have a wife? He barely had time to sleep. How could he devote himself to love? His planet stood on the brink of war—war with the Federation, conflict with the Cysgodians. Duty and responsibility were cold comforts in the night, and yet that is all he could afford.

The odds that Nova meant more than duty was unlikely. Besides, the elders had always told him that with one's mate, you just knew. A married dragon could hear his wife in his head, sense her, even project images into her mind. It was a connection so deep and powerful that a dragon's long life became the life of his mate.

Kane again looked over Shelter City, wondering where she had gone. He didn't hear Nova in his head. He didn't sense where she was in the city.

Aside from attraction mixed with frustration, there was nothing to support a fantasy of more.

"I'm just lonely," he muttered under his breath, dismissing the daydream.

"How about some company?" Payton appeared next to him.

He had been so preoccupied that he hadn't heard her approach. "Aren't you supposed to be on your way to the palace?"

Payton shrugged. "Was that an order? I thought it sounded more like a suggestion."

"I see now why the gods deigned it necessary to only give shifters male children for so many centuries. The females are much more stubborn than any of us males." Kane gave her a half-smile. Just as his generation was the first male dragons to fly, so was it the first generation that female shifters had been born in great numbers.

Payton laughed and didn't try to deny it. She started to walk to the path that would take them along the cliffside down to the city. "Come with me. I want to hear what happened after I left."

Kane followed her to the incline but said, "I can't. I have been ordered to track Nova. I need to locate her."

"Then come with me," Payton insisted.

She paused beside a large, deformed tree growing on the cliff. The trunk blocked the view from the city and barracks below. The incline beneath the forest hid them from the stronghold facility above. It was the only private area on the path down.

"I saw her go into the city. Yevgen will be able to find her faster with his cameras than we can. He sent word that he has information to share. Could be worth getting your proper dignitary hands dirty by disobeying royal orders."

"It's not disobeying if it's to find Nova," Kane countered. He quickened his pace down the side of the cliff toward the city.

"You really need to get out of the royal offices more." Payton followed him. "Where is your sense of adventure? What happened to the boy who set all the solarflowers on fire and nearly took down the Draig barracks? And then tried to fly away before his parents could stop him?"

Kane chuckled at the distant memory. "I believe he is still locked in his room as punishment. My mother threatened to chain me to the ground."

She never had.

Payton's brow furrowed, and she looked at her feet. "Did I ruin the negotiations?"

"You were forceful in your opinions, but no. I don't think you can be blamed for the outcome." Kane gave her a condensed version of the meeting, skipping over speculation that something was happening between him and Nova.

The soft murmur of indistinct conversation came from below, blended voices of a crowd rising and falling. He could concentrate on them and pick the conversations apart if he wanted. Instead, he let it float like musical notes.

"I'll ask Yevgen to monitor her," Payton said. "He already watches Doyen. Ever since he recorded that speech about shifters living ten times longer than a Cysgodian man and suggested the blood-drinking thing. Gross. Also, he's sexist. There are no women in his group."

"I don't trust a man who can't trust a woman," Kane said by way of agreement.

As they came to the bottom of the path into the city, the conversations lightened. People stopped to watch them.

"It's strange not having to come in disguise," Payton said, keeping her eyes forward. She'd snuck into the city often when it was under Federation rule. "I almost prefer doing so. Now everyone stares."

Kane had not spent much time in the city when the Federation was in charge, but he had watched it from above. Walking through it felt as if he'd stepped onto a different planet.

Pieces of metal were pressed into the dirt, stuck down when it had rained, and then left half buried as they dried. They were meant to be walkways. The sounds of children's feet clanged as they ran over them.

There was no order to Shelter City. The homes butted against each other at odd angles, creating tiny alleyways, many of which went nowhere. Some exterior walls were held together with rope strung between rooftops. Pieces of canvas flapped to create patches of shade.

Roads curved and straightened with no fore-thought in design. From the sky, Kane likened them to rivers. In their imperfection, as a whole, it could be considered beautiful like nature...at least until he took a closer look and saw the underlying poverty that created the shapes. No one should have to live like this.

Steady clangs and taps sounded as a breeze rolled through the streets. The sidewalks turned from metal to wood where vendors stood displaying their wares.

"Two stones," a man demanded payment, "or go elsewhere."

"It's not worth one." A woman threw a piece of canvas at the shopkeeper and marched away.

They continued, though there was an air of uncertainty to their actions. Eyes followed Kane and Payton. Voices hushed. One question seemed to hang unspoken.

What now?

Kane still did not have the answer to that question.

"We'll cut through here." Payton turned between two buildings. The path did not look like an actual walkway, but she easily navigated through it, dipping under a low overhang and inching around narrow corners.

When Payton emerged onto a street, he heard a woman say, "That's one of them. Get inside. Don't make them angry."

Kane wanted to assure the woman that they weren't there to hurt them, but she was already carrying her child inside. A door slammed.

"Don't bother," Payton said. "It's been like that since the rebellion. They're scared of making us angry. Trying to convince them otherwise doesn't help. I've tried."

"I—" A shiver worked over Kane, instantly distracting him. He turned to stare down the street. A few people moved along the shaded path. His vision focused on each of them.

"What is it?"

"Nova. She's here." Kane stepped toward the crowd.

"I don't see her." Payton followed him.

"It's a smell." Kane lifted his hand. "Go to Yevgen. See what he wants to tell you."

He heard more than witnessed Payton striding away.

Kane rushed down the street. The scent had been subtle, and he'd lost it almost as quickly as he'd found it. He felt his blood stirring as the dragon offered to take over the hunt. His flesh tingled, and he had to resist the urge to half-shift. If the locals were already frightened, his dragon didn't need to run wildly through their city.

Two women wheeled a cart full of metal down the middle of the street. The intermittent screeches of the axle sounded like tiny screams. He searched their faces, but they weren't Nova.

His heartbeat quickened. He came to a cross-roads, turned left, and kept moving.

Nova.

Suddenly, he stopped and ducked against the side of a building. He tried to hide within the shade, knowing she'd see him if she bothered to look in his direction. He focused his attention on her.

"Did you get it?" Nova leaned over, speaking privately to a young girl, who nodded. "You did well, Tanja."

"I did like you said when they were distracted. I brought it to the—" Tanja tried to answer.

Nova covered Tanja's mouth with her hand and shook her head. "No. Don't say it. No one can know where it's hidden. Not even me."

Tanja nodded.

Nova lowered her hand from the girl's mouth. "Trust no one. Many lives depend on this. No faction leaders. Don't use it for tributes or trades. No one can know you have it. I'm trusting you."

Tanja again nodded. "I promise."

Kane frowned, wondering what they were hiding. He tilted his head, straining to hear their whispers.

"You know where I keep my key," Nova said. "I won't be there much, but you'll be safe."

"Did you go to the...?" The girl turned to look toward the stronghold over the city. "Did they ask about me? Did the drone see me?"

Nova shook her head. "No. They don't know about you."

Kane frowned. Was this her daughter? Someone else she was hiding from them? Why?

"But I—"

"Didn't do anything," Nova interrupted. "You were never there."

Tanja looked as if she wanted to discuss it, but Nova shook her head.

"I was there. I did something," Nova stated. "Not you."

"But..."

"Say you weren't there," Nova ordered.

"I wasn't there."

Nova put her hands on Tanja's shoulders. "You protected me. Thank you. In this life, all we have is our people and our loyalties. Everything can be lost if we're not careful. Never forget."

Tanja nodded. "I won't."

"Now, go." Nova gave her a gentle nudge. "Be safe. Head down. Eyes alert."

Tanja took off, running toward a short wall. She jumped onto a ship part on the ground and used it to propel her body over. Kane heard soft thumps as the girl kept going.

Nova hung her head and took a deep breath.

Holding it for a long moment, she simply stood. Kane found himself inching closer to her. The moment reminded him of when he found her alone on the cliff by the watchtower. There had been something sad about her that called to him. He'd been worried she was thinking of doing something terrible to herself, but more than that, he wanted to hear her voice. He'd thought about her quite a bit since the rebellion.

The women with the cart returned. The squeak of their wheel lighter but still announcing their arrival. Kane glanced to find they pulled an empty cart.

When he turned his attention back to Nova, she had gone.

8

Nova ran through the maze of back alleys, ducking between buildings to find a decent hiding place. What was Prince Kane doing following her? The shock of seeing him hiding in the shadows (not very well but hiding) had caused her stomach to tighten in fear.

How much had he heard?

Damn shifter hearing. She should have known better than to speak to Tanja in the open. The street had been mostly empty, though, and she'd thought it would be all right to talk.

Please, don't let them know what she did. Blame me. Punish me.

Nova wasn't sure who she prayed to or if anyone beyond the reality of Shelter City would even care.

People spoke to gods, but they had never answered back.

She thought of the drone. What had it seen? At the time she'd been sure Tanja had been hidden from its view, but each time she thought back, she doubted her memory a little more. What if there had been a second drone? She'd been so focused on the weapon aimed at her.

Nova had no idea what would happen if the Federation could prove Tanja shot a well-connected soldier while he was down—or even if they just suspected but couldn't prove it. The fact that it was an accident wouldn't matter. It wouldn't be the first time someone had disappeared from Shelter City. One day here, the next day...nothing. General Sten had imprisoned people for much less.

Nova couldn't lose another person she cared about.

That the shifters all seemed worried about retaliation by the Federation revealed much. They had a weakness, and she'd threatened it. That is what her mother would have done.

She shouldn't have done it.

She wished she could take it back.

Were they coming after her now?

She didn't want to believe Kane would hurt her.

When she looked into his eyes, she felt as if he spoke honestly. But charmers came in pretty packages. It didn't mean they were trustworthy. It just meant she had to be more careful.

Her mother's words whispered through her mind. *"They might not be an enemy, but they have not proven themselves to be friends."*

Seeing a metal pole leaning against a building, she grabbed it as she passed. She ducked into a small alcove and pressed her back to the wall. Her hands trembled as she held the pole.

Nova had no idea what she was going to do with the weapon, but fear caused her to grip it harder. She'd threatened royalty, and she did it with witnesses from Shelter City. Did she really believe there wouldn't be a retaliation? Their lives would be easier without resistance. Would they take Shelter City into submission by any means necessary?

People disappeared all the time.

She wasn't ready to be nothing.

Nova bit her lip, trying to control the sound of her heavy breathing. When nothing happened, she started to relax her arms. The pole lowered to her side.

Like many hidden nooks in the city, the alcove was constructed at odd angles from the sides of buildings. Faded red, blue, and yellow paint held patches of rust. The mishappen overhang of roofing material cast a shadow, and she inched beneath it to better hide.

The impression of footprints marred the dirt. Someone had been exploring. The children especially liked to find secret forts. She heard shouts from the city, the constant noise that backdropped every day.

Thud. Thud.

The soft sound was barely discernable, and she couldn't be sure if it was her heart pounding, actual footsteps, or her imagination.

Nova tried not to move but ended up turning her head to angle her ear toward the alcove's opening.

Thud.

She held her breath and gripped the pole so hard that her hands began to ache.

Thud.

So soft. It could have been her heart. She lifted the pole, ready to swing.

Motion blurred into the alcove's opening. Her eyes detected the hard, armored flesh of a dragon-man. She didn't think, only acted. Fear caused her to cry out as she swung the pole to protect herself.

The half-dragon caught the pole with one hand before it reached his head and jerked it from her fingers. He tossed it behind him with a growl. Sharp talons at the end of his fingers extended like thick claws.

Nova backed away. She'd seen the dragon-men but never this close, never this helpless and alone. Hardened brown skin covered his body, at least that which wasn't hidden by his clothing. A ridge had formed across the brow and down the center of the forehead to create a protective shield over his nose. Perhaps the most chilling were the yellow eyes staring at her.

No. She was wrong. Not the most chilling.

The dragon opened his mouth to show fangs.

His chest rose and fell as if he panted.

"Kane?" she asked, her voice weak. "Is that you?"

Nova had a feeling it was, but she couldn't be sure in this form. His clothes matched the tunics many of the dragons wore. She trembled in fear. Why had she picked this hiding spot? There was no other outlet from the alcove, and her only weapon had been defeated with ease.

How could she fight a dragon? One swipe of his hand, and that would be it.

"Prince Kane?" She used his title, hoping to show respect. Royals liked deference, right? "May I help...?"

Her words trailed off. It was a stupid question. Of course she couldn't help him.

He stepped forward, and she stumbled backward. The sound of her ragged breath mingled with his more controlled pants. The narrow space made the sound abnormally loud.

He took another step.

"Please," she whispered. "Don't."

The word reminded her of the cliffside when he had told her not to jump.

"Don't," she repeated. What if the animal didn't understand her? She didn't know how shifting worked. Maybe the man inside couldn't hear her. She needed to reach him. "Kane. Don't."

His hand lifted, slowly, taloned fingers outstretched. He came closer, and she couldn't force her legs to move. She stiffened as he made contact with her face.

The hard warmth of armored flesh let her know his true strength. The sharp tips touched her ear but didn't pierce into her skin. His thumb moved along her cheek, stroking her, sliding in a tear she hadn't realized had fallen.

Nova did not expect the gentleness and wasn't sure what to do. She stared into his yellow eyes and whispered the only word that would leave her lips. "Don't."

He closed his eyes. The hand against her skin softened, the tip of a talon sliding lightly against her as it retracted. She watched the shift from dragon to man move up his arm, the armor becoming buried in firm male flesh. The change worked its way up his neck to his jaw. His trim beard appeared to grow. His nose emerged and began to reshape his handsome face. The ridge over his brow receded into his forehead. As Kane's familiar face emerged, he opened his eyes. Yellow faded into green.

He still touched her. She had thought the man would be easier to face than the dragon, but the fear remained. Even in this form, she couldn't fight him. Not without a weapon.

"I would never hurt you, Nova," he said, the words hoarse.

She wondered at the sentiment, wanting to trust it but unsure.

"You..." She couldn't finish a thought as her mind raced. His touch did something to her, filling her with awareness—awareness of their power dynamic, of his nearness, of the seclusion in which they'd found themselves. No one would heed her screams in the already loud city. Even if they searched, they wouldn't find her.

"I would never hurt you," he repeated, the words strong and firm as if he needed her to hear them. "Don't fear me."

The fear began to ease, unlocking her brain from its grasp, but the adrenaline remained. It pumped through her veins, heightening all her senses. Every part of her was aware of every part of him.

"Why are you following me?" Nova didn't pull her cheek from his touch. She couldn't. The connection burned into her, and she could no more remove it than she could leave her own skin.

"I was ordered to," he answered. At least it was honest.

"Why?"

"Because the others fear what you will do." Kane's thumb stroked her ever so slightly. A wave of longing rushed through her, centering in her stomach.

"I was angry. I just want to protect my people. I don't want anyone else to die." The words just came out, and she didn't even consider lying. "I know we're not wanted anywhere in this universe. Please just let us keep this piece, this tiny piece. We don't have anything else."

He moved closer, the movement measured and slow. His eyes remained fixed on hers.

"No." Kane shook his head in denial. Nova's chest tightened. "That's not right. You are very much wanted."

His admission surprised her, and she gasped. Kane leaned his mouth to hers, and she met his kiss. Simmering passion erupted between them. The kiss instantly deepened.

She hadn't expected this. Him.

Nova reached for him. Her fingers wound along the back of his neck to hold him to her. The softness of his beard tickled.

The contact felt amazing, and it pulled her in. Nova wanted more. She wanted to be held and feel cherished, even if the moment was fleeting. So much of her life had been alone in a crowded space.

Don't. Her mind whispered the word like a plea. She wasn't sure if it was an internal warning or the only thing it could come up with. Their word. *Don't.*

Don't jump.

Don't leave.

Don't stop.

"Don't stop," she said against his mouth.

A strong arm wrapped her waist, pulling her hard against his body. The firm hold left no question of his desire. The impression of it pushed into her through the thinness of his clothing.

"Uh, Kane?"

Nova opened her eyes in surprise at the feminine voice intruding on their alcove and pulled away from the kiss. Kane gazed at her, the green swirling with yellow. It took a moment for his gaze to clear, and his brow furrowed.

The woman continued, "When you're done with your interrogation, I need you to join me. There are some things you need to see."

Nova jerked her hands away from his neck and stepped back. His hands lingered on her cheek and back, flexing several times before finally releasing her.

Bitter reality flooded her.

What was she doing?

What were *they* doing?

He was a shifter prince. She was the leader of the Revolutionists. They didn't belong together. They couldn't belong together. No one would understand.

Nova didn't exactly understand.

She'd seen the way people looked at Justina for marrying a shifter. It was impossible not to hear the jokes made at the woman's expense. Even Nova had judged the woman for it.

Nova felt the impression of his kiss lingering on her lips. She wanted more. Her body wasn't done. Unfulfilled desire surged in an angry panic. Her mouth wanted more of the sensation. Her hips did not want to be denied their pleasure. Her back wanted his hands to roam. Her legs wanted to be lifted off the ground.

By all that was sacred, she wanted him.

She wanted him.

Oh, blackest of holes, she wanted him.

"What is it, Payton," Kane finally answered. His eyes stayed on Nova, watching her intently.

She couldn't have him.

"Yevgen. He found some things," Payton answered, her voice becoming slightly less muffled. Nova saw the princess appear from around the corner as if she had been waiting for them to stop kissing.

"It can't wait?" Kane still didn't look at the woman. His hands flexed as if he could still feel Nova on this flesh.

"Would I be here if it could?" Payton put her hands on her hips and waited. "Bring her along."

Kane motioned for Nova to walk with him. She didn't feel as if she had a choice. She couldn't outrun one shifter. Two would be impossible, and Payton might not be so forgiving when she caught her. The woman clearly had a temper if her outburst at the meeting was any indication. She'd also defied her king, as she had not returned to the Var palace as ordered.

"You couldn't have waited?" Kane grumbled. "How did you find us?"

"Yevgen found her. Or did you forget we were supposed to be looking?" Payton nodded at Nova, obviously not concerned that she listened to everything she said. "When I left to run here, she was waiting to hit you with a pole. How was I to know what you would be doing two seconds later?"

Nova didn't speak. There was nothing she wanted to say. She glanced around the alcove, wondering if a drone had come by and she'd been too distracted to hear it.

Payton led the way back out of the maze of alleys. The princess set a fast pace and didn't look back to make sure they followed. Nova saw the pole weapon laying on the ground but didn't bother to go for it.

Kane gestured for Nova to walk beside him. She felt him looking at her, but she kept her eyes on Payton. She wasn't exactly a prisoner, but she also wasn't free to leave.

They made their way back to the street where the chase had started. Payton leaped over the fence blocking the path with ease.

Kane threaded his hands and offered them to her. "Put your foot on. I'll help you over."

Nova had been navigating the city for years. She ignored the hands and gave a small run toward the sidewall. Her foot hit a notch in the wood, and she used it to propel herself to the other side. Seconds after she landed, Kane launched over the side and landed on both feet next to her.

"Yevgen likes his privacy," Payton told Nova.

Nova wasn't sure what she was supposed to say to that.

Payton glanced around before saying to Kane. "Put your shirt over her head as a blindfold."

Nova stepped back and shook her head in denial. "I'm not doing that."

"I can always summons the cat-shifter guard to come wait with you while we go," Payton offered.

"It won't be long." Kane pulled his shirt over his head. Nova remembered the feel of that chest against her. He handed it to her.

She reluctantly took it, frowning as she wrapped the material around her head. The warmth of his body had infused the shirt, along with his scent. It ignited the desire she had already tried to tame.

Kane touched her arm. "I'm going to carry you. It'll be faster."

Nova shook her head, but her body was already in motion. Her feet lifted from the ground. She made a soft noise of surprise before settling next to his chest. He cradled her in his arms, looping behind the back of the knees. If the warmth from his shirt ignited her senses, being against his chest set her whole body on fire.

Nova opened her eyes to try to peek. She saw only a tiny thread of light along the bottom edge. She held her breath, trying to focus on anything that wasn't Kane.

The task proved to be impossible.

Kane began to jog.

"Come back. Don't interfere," she heard a man order. The sound of running feet followed the command. A father must have been telling his children not to get involved with what the shifters were doing. "It's none of our concern."

Suddenly, he stopped and lowered her to the ground. Nova wobbled on her feet, not ready to be let go. He steadied her by her arm.

"I'm going to lead you in," Kane said. He guided her gently by her elbow.

Kane helped her navigate between two metal barriers. The light from the bottom of the shirt blindfold darkened. They were forced to turn to the side as the path narrowed.

"We're turning," Kane said. The light disappeared altogether. "Step up."

She followed his words, as well as the movements she sensed through his touch.

Kane tugged the shirt from her head to reveal they did indeed move through darkness. He pulled it over his head and redressed.

A soft knock sounded ahead of them before blue light shone as Payton opened a door. The entryway was a piece of old wood on hinges. With the ease in which it opened, she wondered where they could have gone in the city. If the man liked privacy, his entryway must have been well hidden.

Payton and Kane stepped into the flickering

blue light. Nova hesitated, inching forward as she looked inside.

The way the walls cut together appeared like an outdoor alcove. The odd angles and colors told her they were exterior walls to other buildings. Overhead, thick material covered the hideout. It blocked out all sunlight. Not even a sliver managed to stream through.

"What is this place?" Nova asked, coming fully inside. The light came from a wall of monitors. Views of Shelter City flickered on each one, the screens moving as if to monitor the entire city in a matter of seconds. She even saw a picture of the barracks and the Federation stronghold. With each flicker, the muffled sounds of those onscreen changed.

The largest monitor was the only screen not changing. People walked by a busy street next to a marketplace. Nova frowned, leaning closer. She knew that place. She had never seen drones there recording.

Payton shut the board door. "Yevgen, I brought Kane and—"

"Nova," a voice finished.

The large monitor flashed to show her picture. Her mouth hung open, and her eyes squinted like she had been about to sneeze. Nova frowned, not comfortable with the idea of being watched by this Yevgen.

Metal casters rolled along a ceiling track as a man came from the darkness behind the screens. He hung from a sling. The shape of his body was shadowed in darkness, but she saw his legs dangling and his arms poking from the sides of the moving chair.

"Yes," Payton said. "We hid the path from her, and we'll make sure she can't find her way back."

Yevgen came into the blue light so she could better see him. Cyborg eyes met hers. Mechanical irises whirled and focused on her. The screen flashed to show a new picture had been added of her face. Seeing her hair sticking up from where the shirt had been over her head, Nova automatically smoothed it down. The surprised expression her new picture wore wasn't much better.

"Come get these," Yevgen said to Payton. The princess automatically went to him and twisted his leg with a hard jerk. The limb popped off with a fizzling noise. Payton removed the second leg the same way.

"They're almost there. The programming is not quite right," Yevgen said as Payton carried the legs behind the monitor wall. She returned seconds later without them. "Thank you, my love."

Love? Nova looked from the cyborg to the princess in surprise. Kane chuckled. Payton didn't return Yevgen's sentiment, but she did pat his shoulder lightly as she stepped past.

The cyborg turned in his sling to face the monitors.

"I don't understand. What is this place? How is this here, and nobody knows about it?" Nova asked.

Yevgen pointed toward the ceiling. "Tech shields. Protected me from the Federation census."

"Yevgen, can you bring up the videos for Kane?" Payton asked, her tone softer than anytime Nova had heard it.

"Yes. Under the terms already established for the trade," Yevgen stated

Nova again reappeared onscreen. This time she was mid-stride. She gasped and quickly backed toward the door. She bumped into Kane. He caught her by her arms, and she instantly pulled free and turned to keep them all in her sights.

Payton arched a brow but didn't give chase.

"I'm not for trade," Nova stated. "Let me out of here."

"No one is going to trade you," Kane assured her.

Yevgen spun around in his sling. He gave her a once-over. Nova crossed her arms over her chest to stop the visual examination.

He turned his back on her in dismissal as if coming to a decision. "I would not accept you if you were."

Nova frowned, slightly offended by the comment. She felt her hair again to make sure it was still smoothed down. Not that she wanted to be traded, but still... A woman had pride.

Yevgen tapped his fingers on the small console in front of the monitors. A series of images appeared. Nova again moved closer to see what he was showing them.

"I heard we need to be ready," a redheaded woman said, huddled in conversation with a brunette. "Immortality."

The screen flashed to a man. "He said it will cure everything, make us immortal. The virus will no longer be dormant. It will disappear."

The broken conversations kept coming, forming a compilation of clips to tell a larger story.

"The virus will be gone," a shopkeeper told his customer.

"No more virus," a boy told a girl as they stood in an alleyway.

"The sickness will disappear from our blood," the same girl told her mother as she settled down onto her floor mat for the night. "Magic."

"There is no magic," the girl's mother dismissed.

"Blood magic," stated a man before handing over stones to pay for his goods.

"You must drink it fresh. Then they can't kill you. Nothing can," a man told a woman in a passionate whisper before lifting her skirts. They were pressed into an alleyway. A shadow of someone walking past did not disrupt their obvious transaction.

The screen stopped on the woman's bored face as the man had started his business.

"There are more," Yevgen stated, not offering to show them.

"Blood magic," Payton told Kane.

Nova felt sick to her stomach. She kept her distance from them as Yevgen pulled up another image. She did not hold out much hope that this conversation would go in her favor.

9

VIRUS CURES AND BLOOD MAGIC?

Kane focused on the monitors, but he stayed aware of Nova's location. The memory of her body against his urged him to move closer. He refrained. Instead, he listened to the cadence of her soft breaths.

Yevgen liked an audience and thrived on the slow divulging of information. The rumors that drinking blood equaled immortality were dangerous speculations. If a desperate mob attacked a lone shifter, the outcome might not be favorable.

Kane shared a look with Payton. "Tell me no one has been attacked over this."

Yevgen gave a slight shake of his head. "Not that I've seen."

"Good," Payton said. "Keep monitoring."

"Keep watching," Yevgen instructed. "I have a new piece you have not seen, my princess."

Doyen appeared wearing a black cloak. He stood before a congregation of followers crammed into a nondescript building. He paced back and forth on a small stage, making a great show of his anger before finally stopping to stare over the crowd. A murmur rose, only to fall just as quickly when he lifted his hands.

Kane heard Nova's breath catch slightly, but she didn't react otherwise.

"How well do you know this Doyen?" Payton asked Nova.

"Not well," Nova said. "More of him."

Payton arched a brow but turned back to the screen. "His crowd is bigger than last time. More people are listening."

"I went up the mountain to the would-be new palace of those shifter kings," Doyen announced, indicating this had just happened.

"They tried to make me dine on their lies." Doyen thrust his palm forward for emphasis as he added, "Tried to cram them down my throat while expecting me to say thank you for the rotten meat tainted by their food simulators."

A loud protest met his words, and he basked in the shouts before lifting his arms to settle them once more. The image distorted briefly, and the sound stuttered.

"They tried to say the blue radiation cured us," Doyen announced. "So they could ship us off to space to die."

"Lies!" a man shouted, hidden within the crowd's numbers.

"Lies," Doyen repeated, pacing for effect. "Do you feel cured? Do you have immortality? If this is true about the blue sun, why the shifters and not us? Why do we age when they do not? Do we not live in its rays, bask in its daylight? Do we not breathe the same air? I believe what I can see. During the battle, how many dead dragons did you witness? How many dead cats did you carry to their graves? How many shifters met a funeral pyre?"

"None," came several answers from various parts of the crowd.

Kane wished just one person in the crowd would question what the man said, poke at the logic of it to see its weakness. No one did. They wanted to believe. Doyen preyed on fear. And those fears gave Doyen great power.

"None," Doyen said. "And how many dead from

Shelter City? How many were murdered by Federation blasters while not one shifter was harmed?" Doyen shook his head. "That is what I have seen, what we have all seen with our eyes. They cannot tell us immortality does not exist because we have witnessed what I have told you to be true all these years."

Shouts lifted before the sound cut out and froze.

"Is that all?" Payton asked.

"I have another view." Yevgen pushed several buttons on his console. It again started to play.

"Cysgodians are dying! Lives shortened. Our children stolen from the future." The screen moved closer to Doyen's face as he continued, "The shifters have stood by doing nothing as the Federation pretended to save us after releasing the virus on our homeworld. How many years have these royals watched as we starved? Our rations cut? Sitting on their watchtowers like we were nothing more than entertainment. Flying down over our city, breathing fire to scatter our people for nothing more than sport?"

Kane's lips pressed together as he fought his anger. That had only happened a few times to stop rioting in the streets. Without intervention, many would have died. The fire had sent them running, and no one had been harmed.

No one spoke as they listened to the horrible speech.

"They fly overhead, mocking us for being trapped in this city of rust while they live in palaces and roam the forest free. They sneak into our city in costume, trying to hide as they witness our despair like tourists."

Kane turned to Nova to see her reaction. Her arms were crossed in front of her chest, and she looked unwilling to move for fear of drawing notice. Her eyes focused on the screen while sounds of displeasure and rage came from the crowd.

"Now that Cysgodian lives have been taken in pursuit of our freedom, *now* they wish to come and offer help? They pretend benevolence, offering medical care and food from devices that will kill us. They say, take these clothes and live in these barracks, but do not leave Shelter City. Do not cross into our territory. Stay and do as you're told!"

The crowd became almost frenzied.

Doyen relished the fury he'd fueled. The shouts stopped as the screen sped forward in time.

This time Doyen's voice had softened. He had the crowd under his spell, and he knew it. "So I went up there, to their newly conquered palace, and told the shifter kings we will not be subjected to their rule. I told them that we had witnessed the deaths of our neighbors and friends. We saw the bodies lining the streets. Our world died. After that, nothing they do to us will scare us. We have lived through the worst nightmare, and we survived."

The crowd went wild, jumping up and down.

Kane again looked at Nova. She still refused to meet his gaze. Those had been her words, paraphrased. Doyen had made no such comments.

"I told them this is *our* home. We don't need their permission. We will choose our own leaders and run our own territory." Doyen's gestures and words grew more grandiose with each passing phrase. "We will have our own king. And beware the shifter that comes onto our land because we will take their immortality with blood!"

Doyen pumped his fist into the air as the crowd picked up a chant. "Blood, blood, blood—"

"Turn it off," Payton said. The screen froze, and the room became quiet.

"That's not what I said," Nova whispered. A shiver worked over her entire body. "He twisted everything."

They stood in silence, staring at the screen. Doyen's gleeful expression stared back.

"That man will never be king," Payton decreed. She looked at Nova, her expression unreadable.

Kane stepped closer to Nova, wanting to shield her from Payton's cold stare.

"Yevgen, please, show him the others," Payton urged.

Lowri appeared on the monitor with a group of women. "Gather your things quietly. We need to claim the largest homes in the barracks before they give them to Revolutionists. They don't need the space like we do. I pretended like we didn't want it so the other factions wouldn't make a run for the best rooms. Once they let us in, find the room you want and refuse to leave. Take your children. The captain's suite is mine. We have an example to set."

Kane dismissed the woman. She wasn't more than a nuisance. The shifters had plans in place to assign the rooms. It would not be a free-for-all.

Next, Gethin and six other Shopkeepers were smuggling food rations crates from a store while a seventh stood watch. None of them spoke, and they moved like they'd done it before.

Neither of the last two events caused concern when compared to other matters. The Shopkeepers' ration stock would have to be exposed, but that was a small matter.

"They stole the rations meant for the southern distribution sector," Nova said. "Several families live in that area with young children. Food is already scarce."

Kane frowned, instantly changing his opinion of the severity of the crime. "We will deal with them. No child will be without food."

"Yevgen, show him," Payton said.

Kane frowned, wondering what else there was to see. Payton glanced at him and appeared apologetic.

"Payton, what—?" Before he could finish, a young voice came from the monitor. His eyes darted to the screen to watch.

"Dragons are scarier because they can fly away after they breathe fire on us, but cats are braver because they stay on the ground and fight face-to-face." The girl Nova had been talking to earlier sat against a wall while Nova dug along the edge of the building. Orange light flashed, and he recognized the glow of dragon fire lighting the area.

Payton chuckled despite herself. "Smart girl."

"Stop." Nova stepped toward the cyborg. "Turn it off."

Yevgen ignored her.

"You have no right to spy on us," Nova insisted.

The screen blipped, and the audio recording became distorted as, onscreen, Nova said, "...plans in place...you to get as many food rations as you can to your best...for you and the other young ones...take care...fend for..."

"The extra drones during battle interfered with transmissions," Yevgen explained, working feverishly on his console. The image sharpened by small degrees.

"...trades for magic potions or vials of shifter blood...immortality," Nova had said to the girl as she continued to stab the dirt with her shovel.

"Kane, no. That's not what I said," Nova insisted.

He glanced at her briefly and was about to answer, but he didn't want to miss the recording. He'd been ordered to find the truth. He needed to watch.

Nova's shovel had disappeared, and she used a laser cutter on the building's wall. The sound became clearer, and faint noises of battle backdropped her words. "Those dragons and cats outnumber us." The screen blipped to show Nova and Tanja pressed to the building looking at the sky. "They don't want us here, and they are under no obligation to take care of us. The last thirty years are proof of that. The Federation will not tolerate this rebellion. We might get rid of General Sten, but they'll send more soldiers. The best we can hope for..."

The recording began flipping across the screen. Nova's digitalized voice repeated, "is to...is to...is to," like a broken drone directive.

Yevgen slammed his hand on the console in a rare show of frustration.

"It's all right." Payton touched the cyborg's shoulder. "Is this why you delayed showing us, because the recording isn't perfect? It doesn't have to be perfect. He needs to see the truth. The truth is all that matters. What you do is very important."

Yevgen calmed and kept working.

Kane felt Nova's hand on his arm, gripping him. "Don't listen to this. That's not what I said."

"I see with my own eyes that it is you," Kane answered, unsure. He wanted to believe the best in her, but she had threatened to use the Federation against them. Was his attraction getting the better of him? Was his judgment clouded? Both shifter kings had insisted she be watched. He trusted his uncle and King Kirill with his life. Did they see something he could not?

"He's done something to my words. Yes, that's me. I said those things, but not like that." Nova pulled on his arm, trying to get him to leave. "Please, stop watching it. I'll tell you what was happening. I'll show you where."

Kane almost gave in to her pleading, unable to resist the insistence in her gaze.

The sound of flesh striking flesh again drew his attention toward the monitors. Nova had her hand balled into a fist as a uniformed Federation soldier fell to the ground.

"Oh," Payton said under her breath. "Good shot."

Nova had stood over the fallen man before glancing around in apprehension.

"I killed him!" Nova blurted, running toward the monitor. She pushed Yevgen's sling out of the way, sending him gliding into Payton. The princess caught herself to keep from tripping. "Me."

Nova held her arms wide and tried to block as many of the images as she could. Blue eyes begged him to help her. Every part of him wanted to stop this, if only to erase that look from her face. But Payton was right. They had to know the truth. Too many lives were at stake.

"Please. Just stop. I killed him," Nova insisted.

"That didn't kill him. The punch wasn't that hard." Payton righted herself and helped Yevgen to stop spinning in circles in his sling. To the cyborg, she said, "Play the whole thing."

"That was—" the girl's voice from earlier reemerged behind Nova.

"We have to hide him," Nova had answered. The sound of dragging followed her words.

"I confess. I did it," Nova insisted.

The images on all the screens changed to mirror the large monitor. Each held a picture of Nova and the girl. When the audio resumed, duplicates of their voices caused a strange chorus of overlapping noise. One of the monitors lagged seconds behind the others.

"What if he wakes up? We should shoot him." The girl picked up the blaster pistol.

Nova shielded the unconscious soldier with her body. "No. We're not like them. We don't do that."

"He was going to take you. I've seen them do it. I know the look."

"Tanja, have the soldiers taken you?"

"I'm too fast." Tanja shook her head in denial. "Not everyone is fast."

"Was it reported? Was it this guy?" Nova had pointed to the soldier.

"They all look the same," Tanja said. "They come from the shadows in their uniforms. In the daylight, it's easier to spot them, but when the dark night comes..."

Kane wanted to be sick. The very notion of taking a woman by force went against the very core of their moral beliefs. Women were to be cherished and respected. A man who violated that covenant was not a man but a monster.

"Which men?" Kane demanded. "We'll call the ships back and make them—"

A blast from the pistol ran out. Nova had cried out in pain.

Nova lowered her arms and hung her head as the recording continued behind her. Weakly, she insisted, "It was me."

Onscreen, Nova fell to the ground. Her hand smacked against the soldier's bloody face, and she recoiled in a panic.

Kane recognized her leg wound. He'd found her moments after this had happened.

Tanja had dropped the weapon. "I didn't—"

The recording stopped.

"Please," Nova whispered, tears in her eyes when she lifted her head. Desperate eyes met his. "Erase it. She's just a child. I'll confess. I know this man had family connections that made him important. Make me an example to the others. Give me to the Federation if you must but leave her out of it."

"Who is this girl to you?" Kane asked.

"Just a girl who was forced to grow up in the rusted playground of Shelter City. Her mother drinks from those stills. Her father is dead. I look after her." Nova went to him and fisted her hands around the material of his tunic. "Let me look after her. I'll confess."

Kane placed his hands over her trembling ones. He wanted to hold her, kiss her. He wanted to tell her not to fear. He would take care of her. He would take care of Tanja. "It was battle. The rules change in battles. Soldiers died. Cysgodians died. No one person should be punished for fighting. To me, it looked like an accident."

"The Federation won't care. A Cysgodian killed a soldier," Nova insisted. "If this man's family wants justice..."

"The Federation doesn't have this footage," Yevgen stated, sounding almost proud of the fact.

Payton pushed Yevgen back into place so he could resume working.

"It's not the death," Payton clarified. "It's the words."

An image of Nova's face appeared on one side of the monitors and Doyen's on the other. Nova stepped to the side to watch what they revealed. Her movement turned him slightly while he still had hold of her hands against his chest. The still images flashed from one to the next, each depicting the pair younger than the last. He watched as Nova aged in reverse until decades had passed.

"No," Nova whispered.

The large monitor finally showed a picture of Nova and Doyen together. They each held the hands of a woman. The adult's face wasn't onscreen as Yevgen focused on the children.

"Mother?" Nova whispered, tugging to be free. "That's..."

Kane released her. She went to the screen and touched her mother's image.

"Let me see her face," Nova pleaded. "Please."

Yevgen brought up a picture. The quality wasn't great, but Nova stroked it like it was the most beautiful thing she'd ever seen. He could see the resemblance between the three. How had he missed it before? Same dark hair, the same color of eyes. Their features differed, but if he studied them, he could make the connection.

"Ah, look at her. She was already sick," Nova

said. "She didn't tell us, but you can see how thin she'd become. Even on the ship over, there wasn't enough food, but she always shared hers with us. She said she wasn't hungry, but it must have been a lie. We were all hungry."

"Doyen is your brother," Kane stated. "You said you didn't know him."

That is what Payton wanted him to see. Nova and Doyen were siblings. Nova had lied to him, and he'd believed her. He'd wanted so badly to believe her. Needed to.

First it was Doyen's speech, then Nova's words to Tanja about a plan, and all of it combined into evidence of their plot against the shifters.

Nova dropped her hand from her mother's face. "Only by birth. We're not close. Coming to Shelter City infected his mind. He never fully adjusted to the truth of it. We all wanted our old lives back, but we eventually accepted our place. He couldn't. He thought he deserved more. Our mother was the leader of the Revolutionists. Our father was a respected doctor. Here, we're Federation livestock... well, now just livestock. I suppose you could say I'm ashamed of my brother and who he has become. And I'm positive he feels I should be more respectful of his ego."

"You have the same ideas," Payton countered.

"I already said that recording cut off my words. If you're not going to believe me, there is nothing I can do to change that." Nova looked defeated. "I'm tired. Do whatever you're going to do to me."

Kane's instinct warred with logic. He knew what he saw, and he knew what he felt. The two did not align.

"Salena," he stated.

Nova frowned. "I don't know what that is."

"Grier's wife," he answered. "You'll talk to Salena."

Payton looked as if she thought it was a waste of time. Kane didn't care. He wanted to hear the truth from Nova directly, and there was only one way to ensure he did.

He pulled the shirt over his head and handed it to Nova so she could blindfold herself.

"Thank you, Yevgen," Payton said. "Send word when you are ready to move or if you hear anything else."

"I'll keep my ear to the mud, my princess," the cyborg answered. "But unless you're ready to give me the stronghold, I'll keep my home. I don't wish to leave it."

Payton moved to follow him.

"Please remind Roderic he promised to come back and answer all of my questions about the old ways—nef, marsh farmers, and animal prowess," Yevgen called after them. "I have not forgotten."

"I'll remind him," Payton answered as Kane led Nova through the door into the dark entryway.

10

Nova hated the white walls of the
Federation facility. As much as she longed for a
home that did not leak air and sunlight, that smelled
clean and not of dirt floors, this was worse. This box
of a room with a cot and door was more of a prison
than Shelter City. The locked door didn't respond to
her attempts to open it. Every time she pressed her
palm to the hand scanner it made an ugly noise and
blinked red.

Kane had offered to stay with her throughout
the night while they waited for the arrival of
Princess Salena. He would stand watch while she
rested. Nova had refused. She'd asked for this cell.
She wanted to be alone.

When she looked at Kane, she resented his

mistrust even as she understood it because she mistrusted him too. She also distrusted her feelings when he touched her. She would have kissed him again if he had stayed with her through the night. If they kissed, her treacherous body would not have been able to stay away from him.

Sex would complicate what she needed to do and who she needed to be. None of this was about her feelings. Her feelings didn't matter.

Being compared to Doyen stung. It had been years since she'd even thought of him as her brother. In her head, her family was all dead. That lie she'd told herself had let her hold on to a remnant of good memories.

The bed was firm but comfortable compared to a mat on the floor. Kane had brought her a sealed ration pack for her dinner. She appreciated that he didn't try to force her to eat a food simulator meal.

She also welcomed the clean tunic shirt and loose pants they had given her. Their beige color contrasted the white walls, barely. The new shoes fit a little snug, or maybe they simply weren't falling apart.

Kane had appeared surprised when she said yes to a decontaminator. It would have been humorous had her situation not been so dire. She wasn't a technophobe. She did bathe. Decontaminators cleaned dirt. Medical booths and food simulators altered molecules, an entirely different matter.

A familiar knock sounded, and she instantly knew Kane waited on the other side. The times he'd entered, he always waited for a respectful interval before opening the door—like she would be busy doing something in her white box.

Nova sat on the bed and waited. The door slid open, and Kane entered. He'd changed his clothes. Somehow, to see him in colors made him appear more royal. Embroidery lined the edge of his neck, decorating his blue tunic. Tight black pants fit snugly to his legs.

"She's here," he stated. "Are you ready?"

"To be judged by this Salena?" Nova gave a humorless laugh as she stood from the bed and moved to follow him. "Sure. Let's do it."

Kane blocked the door. The room felt smaller with him in it. The thoughts of him that had tried to surface in the night returned to taunt her. She glanced at his chest, remembering how it looked without the shirt. She recalled the feel of it pressed against her.

"It's not to judge you. It's to learn the truth." His words were soft, and he looked at her as if he knew her response to him. "It is the best way to common ground."

Nova nodded. "I'm ready."

She told herself she wasn't frightened. It was a lie.

"You don't have to be scared. Salena is a good woman." Kane stepped out of the room.

Nova frowned. Her fear must have shown on her face. She would have to be more careful with her expressions. They didn't need to know what she was thinking. Whatever Salena asked her, she was determined to tell whatever truth she could in the shortest way possible. And, if there was something she didn't want to answer, she wouldn't. They might have taken over Shelter City, but they didn't own her thoughts.

Be diplomatic. Don't lose your temper.

Her eyes strayed down as Kane walked in front of her.

Don't stare at the dragon's ass. This is a serious day.

Her treacherous eyes did not lift.

After several paces, his waist twisted slightly. Her gaze darted up to meet his. A half-smile formed on his mouth, but he didn't comment on having caught her.

Nova pointedly watched the edge of the hallway as they walked. They turned through passageways that didn't differ in design. Each closed door looked like a choice in the afterlife, as if to whisper, *What will your fate be? No need to choose wisely. All roads lead to the same place. Nothing you do matters.*

"Nova?" Kane asked.

She realized she'd stopped and stared at a door handle. Her hand had lifted as if she was about to go inside.

"They're this way." This time, Kane waited for her to join him instead of walking ahead of her. "I wish you'd trust me."

"I wish you'd believe me," she responded, her tone more matter-of-fact than his. "I wish all the shifters would believe us."

"After this meeting, relations between you and us shifters should improve," he said.

They put a lot of faith in this Salena's conversational abilities. Unless...

Nova stopped. "What is Salena's deal? Her... specialty? What does she do?"

"She is a Draig princess. Someday she will be queen, but hopefully not too soon," Kane said. "My uncle and aunt are in good health."

"Sure, but what does she do?" Nova insisted.

"She extracts the truth from people." Kane gestured for her to continue. "They're waiting."

"Torture?" Nova demanded.

At that, Kane's expression darkened. "Do you really believe I would let anyone hurt you?"

"How should I know what you would do?" Nova shook her head. "And that wasn't an answer."

"No. No one will lay a finger on you." Kane's mood did not lighten. "It's a conversation."

Nova wanted to believe him. Actually, she *needed* to believe him, or her legs wouldn't have been able to take another step. She slid her feet forward a few times before she stopped shaking enough to be able to walk.

Kane opened the door to the conference room and stepped aside to let her pass. King Ualan and Prince Grier waited next to a woman Nova had never met. They stared at her, not talking.

Justina sat at the far end of the table. Her husband wasn't with her, but King Kirill hovered nearby. The woman smiled, the only face showing kindness. Nova couldn't return the expression.

Thankfully, Payton wasn't there. She didn't think she could handle the outspoken woman's accusatory looks.

"Lady Nova," King Ualan acknowledged. He gestured toward the chairs. "Please."

Lady? Was he mocking her?

Though the request had all the makings of civility—a pleasant tone, a non-threatening gesture—this did not feel like a simple conversation. Interrogation would be a more apt description.

Kane touched her elbow as if to escort her. Nova stepped forward on her own and took the same chair she had sat in during their first meeting.

Her heart beat fast, and she was thankful for the seat. She wasn't sure how much longer her legs would hold her. Kane stared at her, trying to get her attention with the directness of his look. She instead looked at the mystery woman. Was this the famous Salena?

The woman looked regal, beautiful. Something in her brown eyes exuded calm. Long brown hair was pulled into an intricate braid along the nape of her neck. The fitted tunic looked Draig in style. Tiny dragons had been embroidered down the arm of one sleeve.

Be diplomatic. Don't lose your temper. Short answers.

"This is Princess Salena," Kane said, confirming her assumption.

Salena sat down across from her and folded her hands on the table. All she did was study Nova for a long moment, searching her face.

Nova glanced up at Kane in confusion. He was the only one standing on her side of the room.

"Is this it? You just stare at me?" Nova asked.

"Do you resent the shifters?" Salena asked bluntly.

Nova arched a brow. Really? That was her question? Like Nova was really going to fall into the trap of saying—

"Yes."

Blasted stars! Yes? Wrong answer.

Nova pressed her lips together. Why had she said that?

The shifters shared a look. Grier whispered to his father. Salena lifted her hand without turning around, and Grier instantly stopped talking.

Salena kept staring at her. "Why?"

OK, *that* she was not going to answer. Nova tried to hold back.

"Thirty years," Nova stated.

What in the ever-loving black hole universes was happening? Why was she answering this woman?

"Explain," Salena prompted.

No.

"We waited for thirty years, needing help. Shifters said we could come. They gave us a safe haven. Then they watched our suffering." Nova pushed up from the table. Her chair skidded on the floor. She backed away from Salena. "What is this? What are you doing to me?"

"Ask her about the blood magic," Ualan prompted.

Nova frowned. "I don't know anything about blood magic."

"What can you tell us about blood magic?" Salena's gaze didn't waver.

"It's a rumor that's been around for years. People think drinking shifter blood will give them immortality. It's gained traction recently, but it's nonsense." Nova covered her mouth, trying to stop the flow of words. She backed against the wall.

"I told you, she spoke the truth. Yevgen did not get the entire conversation." Kane sounded vindicated.

Nova dropped her hands. Kane had defended her to his family? Why had he not admitted as much to her?

He angled the chair to offer Nova her seat back. "Ask her what she was doing with Tanja."

"Ask me yourself. I'm right here," she quipped in irritation, not returning to the table as she stayed against the wall.

"What were you doing with—?"

Before Salena could finish, Nova answered, "We were trying to steal food rations for after the rebellion. Regardless of which side won, there was a good chance that food distribution would be disrupted. Much planning has been put into different scenarios. I didn't want to use Tanja for it, but I needed someone I could trust. She'd keep the food safe for the children and only the children. I wasn't even supposed to know where she hid it. Then the soldier, Mure, came. He interrupted what we were doing."

Nova kept talking, knowing she should shut up and unable to stop the flow of words whenever Salena prompted her for more information. She told them every detail she could remember of Mure's death, of seeing Kane in his dragon form and waking up in the makeshift medical facility being tended to by Kane's mother. She talked about her fear in a way she would never admit to anyone.

These were her feelings, and they were extracting them from her.

Kane had lied. He had said they weren't going to torture her, but this was worse.

"What do your followers want?" Justina's soft voice was barely audible.

Salena repeated the woman's question.

"Freedom." Nova sighed as she resigned herself to the process. She finally went back to the chair. It was either that, or she'd slide down the wall onto the floor. She stared at her hands. "To be self-sufficient. We want food in abundance and shelter that doesn't creak with floors that don't turn to muck when it rains too much. We want to do this without the risk of health complications. We don't want to reactivate the virus, which is what the Federation soldiers had told us would happen if we accept simulator food or use too many medical units."

Not for the first time, Nova considered they'd been lied to. But how could she risk encouraging her people to eat something that could wipe them out? Many people believed it to be true for so long that they would resist any change to the contrary. Plus, they had seen the unreasonable aggression and the illnesses from those who'd dined on smuggled fare.

"I have two sisters," Salena said.

Nova frowned, wondering where the woman was going with the comment.

"One is happy and married. She was missing, but she lives here now." Salena smiled briefly, but the expression didn't reach her eyes. "The other one is still missing. I know how complicated sibling relationships can be, and I know how private. I also know how difficult it is to talk about, especially when the situation is complicated. So I'm sorry for having to ask you to talk about your brother."

"Then don't," Nova begged. She turned to Kane. "Just believe what I already said."

"I believe you," Kane answered.

"Salena," Ualan urged.

"Tell us about your relationship with your brother, Doyen," Salena said.

It wasn't a question, but that didn't seem to matter. Whatever power Salena's voice possessed, Nova had to answer her if the woman wanted to know something.

She didn't consciously know where to start. Salena had been right. Sibling relationships were complicated, and nothing she would talk about in front of these strangers.

"Doyen is broken," Nova's words came out on their own without her realizing what she would say in advance, "and some cracks cannot be mended. In school, he'd been the smartest in his class. Our father had taken pride in his only son. Every day our mother told him he was special and meant for great things. They said the same to me, but it resonated differently. I was to inherit the role of Revolutionist leader. That had been set. There was no other path for me."

She took a deep breath. Long-buried memories scratched their way to the surface. The others stayed quiet, listening. She wished one of them would scream and distract from the conversation so she could stop talking.

"But with Doyen, they had told him that he could be anything. They said he could sit in the highest position of power on Cysgod, a position I was to help secure for him in my role. He still believes it's my duty to help him ascend to power. He actually said it the last time we talked. I laughed at the notion. I shouldn't have. He'd cracked a little more."

Nova hung her head as a tear slipped over her cheek.

"It's my fault he's saying the things he is. I told him about the blood magic rumor when he was young. I embellished it. Maybe it was to scare him. Maybe it was to give him—*I don't know*—a strange sense of hope. Maybe it was just a story to captivate his attention and distract him from the hunger. I never thought he'd turn it into this."

Nova had told many stories in her youth, just as the children of Shelter City did now. Fantasies made their world tolerable. They made up stories about the one night of darkness a year. There were tales of dragon treasure hidden in the towers if only someone were brave enough to quest to the top. Thankfully, no one had been caught taking that dare.

"Is your brother dangerous?" Salena asked.

Nova nodded. "Yes."

"Would he kill a shifter?" Salena leaned to the side as if trying to get Nova to look at her.

Nova tucked her head down a little more. A tear slid down her face and dripped on her lap. "Yes."

"Can he be reasoned with?" Salena reached a hand across the table. The gesture worked to get Nova to glance up.

Nova shook her head in denial. "I don't know. He's my brother. I love him. I want to believe he can be saved, but I don't know."

Nova trembled and swiped at her eye. She had not been able to admit her love for her sibling even to herself, and now she was forced to say it to them. Kane tried to touch her shoulder, and she jerked her arm away from the comfort he offered. She didn't want their sympathy. She wanted to be left alone.

"Please, no more," Nova begged. She felt so exposed, so ashamed.

"Do you know of any plot to rise up against the shifters? To do us harm with the Federation?" Salena asked.

"No. I was bluffing. No one wants the Federation back. We just want leverage so we can be left alone." Nova again swiped at her eyes. "You can't possibly need anything else from me. I want to go home."

"That's enough," Kirill said. "She's not a threat."

Salena sighed and leaned back in her chair. She closed her eyes and took several deep breaths, holding them a few seconds before letting go.

Kane sat next to her. "You see what she can do. So you know she'll pull the truth from people whether they want her to or not."

Nova studied his face.

"Salena, ask me about the food simulators and medical booths," Kane requested.

Salena opened her eyes and furrowed her brow. She did as he requested.

Kane kept his gaze on Nova as he answered, "The food simulators are safe. The Federation lied about the radiation. The sickness was from eating too quickly and too much after years of hunger. The aggression came from a drug the Federation smuggled into the city. A vendor we call Yellow Shirt admitted he had stolen the food simulators shifters hid in the forest and then spiked the food with the drug. Everything we told you was true. The food is safe. The medical booths are safe. We want to help."

Nova felt sick to her stomach. Even if she believed them, her followers would never believe her.

"Maybe shifters are immune to the princess' power," Nova whispered, wanting to trust the earnest looks on their faces.

"That's easily proven." Salena smiled. "Kane, how do you feel about Nova?"

11

KANE LOOKED AT SALENA IN SURPRISE AT THE question. He hadn't expected it. All eyes turned to him. Grier didn't try to hide his laughing smile, though he did suppress the sound of his chuckle. Salena attempted to look innocent, but he saw a thread of mischief.

"I..." He tried to resist on instinct. This was not the place for this conversation. He had not yet worked out his feelings. Still, he was compelled to answer. "I can't stop thinking about her."

He turned to Nova. She stared at him, her mouth slightly agape as if she too was caught by surprise.

"I can't stop thinking about you." Kane moved

closer. "About that kiss in the alley when you tried to hit me with a pole."

"What?" Grier asked before laughing out loud. "She hit you for kissing her?"

"Shh," Salena shushed her husband.

"He must not be doing it right," Grier teased.

"Let him speak," Ualan scolded his son.

Kane ignored his cousin as he kept talking. He couldn't stop and wasn't sure if he wanted to.

"The first moment I saw you injured in the city, I had to fly down to you," he continued. "And I haven't stopped thinking of you since. I don't have a crystal. I lost it, so I haven't been sure if I should say anything to you. When I saw you at the cliffside, I had to fly down to you again. I think I'll always fly to you."

Nova continued to stare at him with the same stunned look.

"Nova, I want you to trust me." He wanted to touch her, but her expression gave nothing away. "I want you to see me. I want to kiss you. I want to—"

"That's enough," Salena interrupted, clearing her throat. "Embarrassing Kane is the best way I can prove to you that my gift works on shifters. He'd never say that in front of us."

Grier kept laughing. Kane knew he would not

be hearing the end of this. Everyone in the family would know by the end of the day.

Justina's smile was less teasing and more wistful.

His uncle grinned and gave a small nod of approval. "Your parents will be pleased."

Kirill nodded at him as if to say, "Well done, dragon."

Kane waited for Nova to respond. She looked at the others in turn but didn't meet his gaze.

"Am I free to leave?" Nova asked.

"Thank you for speaking to us, my lady," Ualan said.

Nova stood. Her movements were measured as she walked past Kane to the door.

"Nova?" Kane asked when she didn't acknowledge him. Her demeanor worried him, and he imagined he felt sadness coming from her.

She paused at the door, her hand ready to push it open.

"I accept what had to happen because a leader must sacrifice, but if you ever do this to one of my followers, I will not be so understanding. Do not take my compliance today as a weakness. We will resist you if we must." Nova turned to look at Salena in challenge. "Tell me, am I lying?"

Nova didn't wait for an answer before leaving. He heard her feet moving down the corridor.

Kane hesitated, unsure what to do. Nova wasn't sad. She was livid.

"I should never have agreed to this," he said. "I told you I thought she was telling the truth."

"You didn't tell us you love her." Ualan walked around the table.

"I didn't say that," Kane countered. He hadn't said the word love.

"You did, using different words," Grier said, no longer teasing.

"You didn't have to say it." Ualan faced his nephew. "If she is your fate, she will forgive you. It will be determined by the gods. Have faith."

"Harder beginnings make for better marriages," Kirill offered. "We cats do not have crystals to tell us what all shifters already know. You don't need the stone. When you come together, you will feel the truth of it. No other path will make sense."

"This is not the time." Kane stared past his uncle to the door. It was partly fear talking. "The Federation. The factions. There is too much to be—"

Ualan held up his hand. "If she is your mate, she will be welcomed into the family. The rest will be solved."

Kane wanted to take comfort in their words. Yes, for most, fate was decided by the gods and eventually worked out. But there were those sad dragon-shifters whose blessings did not come to fruition. They carried a haunted expression in their eyes, a deep, lonely well that could never be filled. What if he failed to win her?

"Go." Justina pointed at the door.

"She's not pleased. Perhaps she wants to be left alone," Kane said. "I should respect—"

"Of course she's not pleased. Go after her. Let her yell at you. Let her hit you with as many poles as she needs to," Justina persisted. "I can tell you from experience that her existence is not easy. Everything she has, everything she is, has been at risk her entire life. Cysgodians have very few things that are their own. Houses fall. People die. Property is stolen. We live on borrowed land. And now all of that is in chaos with the Federation gone, and they're waiting to see what new hell the overlords will bring because how can it be any different?

"Our history has taught us to expect loss. Her thoughts, those memories, are the only things that belonged to her completely. And though today was a necessity to ensure the safety of this planet, and I see that, I also see what you took from her. So go. If you love her, go. If you have honor, go. Just go, Prince Kane."

Kane felt as if Justina had punched him with a spaceship. His chest tightened, and he couldn't force air into his lungs. No one wanted to share their secrets. He prided himself as a diplomat on seeing things from all angles, but he had missed a significant detail—Nova's profound sense of loss. He'd been so wrapped up in deciphering his feelings, trying to think of ways to prove to his family that she was worthy of being trusted. Never did he question if he was worthy enough to be with her.

His sense of dragon honor had been so ingrained that he never considered that everyone wouldn't automatically see it in him.

Kane rushed out of the doors. He caught Nova's scent and began to give chase. By all the gods, what had he done?

He tracked her to the facility door. Two Var guards stood at the entrance.

"Where?" Kane asked, his voice hoarse. "Where is she?"

One of the guards pointed outside toward the path to Shelter City. "Do you need us to stop her? I thought she was free to leave."

"No. She is free." Kane brushed past the half-shifted cats. He knew those words were a lie. She wasn't free. He wanted her to be. He wanted them all to be, but circumstances weren't allowing for it quite yet.

Kane ran across the clearing toward the path. He had to see her. He had to say something.

No, he had to listen.

For the first time in his life, Kane had absolutely no idea what to do. Fear gripped him, and he forced his steps to slow as he strode down the cliffside path. He couldn't make the wrong decision.

He thought of those lonely, haunted dragons and did not want that to be his fate.

Worse than that, he did not want to be the cause of Nova's pain.

At that moment, he knew he'd choose eternal loneliness if it would bring her even the smallest piece of happiness.

Kane found her hidden behind the large mishappen privacy tree where neither those above nor below could see her. She stood with her back to him, her head down as she took several deep breaths. Her hand pressed against the bark, fingers working as if she debated trying to push it down the cliff.

"I'm sorry," Kane managed, knowing those words would never be enough. "You have every right to be angry. Justina says I should let you hit me with poles."

It was not an eloquent speech, nowhere near.

Her head lifted, but she didn't turn to him. Her fingers stilled on the bark.

"I never meant to take more from you." Kane waited, watching every breath, every movement intently for a sign as to how he should proceed.

"Don't," he heard her whisper, the word so soft it could have been mistaken for the breeze.

Kane nodded, even though she could not see, and took a step back. If she wanted to be alone, he would honor that.

"That word says everything about us, doesn't it?" she continued. "Don't."

Kane stopped moving.

"Don't jump." Her head dipped forward, and she shook it with a small laugh that held no humor. "Don't be free. Don't go. Don't keep secrets. Don't trust. Don't feel. Don't kiss. Don't speak. Don't love. Don't. Just don't."

Nova's name formed on his lips, but he told himself to hear her.

"I'm exhausted, Prince Kane." She looked up once more and removed her hand from the tree only to draw it to rub her face. After a few seconds, she turned to look at him. Her eyes were red. Nova wasn't angry. She'd been crying.

He took an involuntary step forward and lifted his arms.

"Don't," she stated, her blue eyes bright with moisture.

He stopped advancing and obeyed.

"Just don't."

12

Nova wished she could erase the emotions flowing inside of her. She'd tried to forget her childhood, all that loss. The present was what mattered. As a leader, she needed to take care of her people. That was her destiny.

Having nothing was easier when there was nothing more to have.

But then Kane happened.

"I think I'll always fly to you."

His words had terrified her. They came with complications attached.

When he'd said them, she had seen the surprised looks on his family's faces and heard the teasing. She'd also glimpsed the reluctance on Kane's. He hadn't wanted to confess. She couldn't blame him. Confessing affection for her would be as embarrassing as her having to tell the Revolutionists about him.

"I'm sorry for what we put you through," Kane said, not coming closer. "I'm sorry for what *I* put you through. It was never my intention to make you cry."

"You didn't make me cry. Memories made me cry. There is a reason people bury the past." Nova stayed within the shade of the large tree, hidden. "That is where my love for my brother resided. Buried. It's where I needed it to stay. I can't save him from himself. Whom I loved doesn't exist anymore. Doyen is just someone I used to know. My family is gone. I need it to remain that way."

"You might find it very little consolation, but now that it's been proven you don't plan on sabotaging relations with the Federation, we know you can be trusted." Kane took the smallest step toward her as if waiting for her reaction. "I hope this means we'll be able to move forward with finding an agreeable path."

"I want to trust you," Nova admitted. However, even if she believed their intentions, the other Cysgodians would not. Fear had taken root long ago and it was in deep.

"Would you like me to get Salena? You can have her ask me anything you wish." He began to turn.

Nova reacted on impulse. She grabbed his arm to stop him. The shock of his warmth against her fingers sent a wave of awareness into her body. "Don't."

The word hung between them as she held his arm. His eyes met her gaze, and she knew before she started pulling him into the shade with her that she would kiss him again. Whatever this feeling was between them, it was stronger than her sense of duty. It surged in great bursts of air, forcing her to go where it wished. She could no longer fight it than she could resist the urge to breathe. She could try to hold her breath, but the burn inside her would become too great, and she would need to gasp for air.

It felt natural for their lips to meet, like the first gasp to soothe a deprived body. They instantly picked up where they'd left off in the alley. Everything faded but that moment. She needed to feel the promise of his touch, no matter how fleeting.

Nova kept ahold of him until her back hit against the bubbly texture of the bark. His body pressed against hers, trapping her. The length of his arousal formed along her stomach.

She broke the kiss, panting for breath. Her

hands roamed his body, exploring everywhere she could reach. Fingers slid up her tunic shirt. He caressed her hips and waist before moving higher to cup her breasts.

Kane moaned as he brought his lips back to hers. Their mouths warred as if each tried to consume the other. His intentions were made clear in each harsh breath and passionate touch.

Nova met his desire with her own. She pushed his pants down his hips, the invitation unmistakable. She wanted this, and she was going to let herself take it.

Kane mimicked her actions, gliding his hands down her hips to free her of the tunic pants. She managed to pull one boot free of a pant leg to rub her thigh against his.

A moment of sanity intruded as she looked around. "Someone might see us."

His gaze flashed with dragon yellow. "I don't hear anyone."

That was all the reassurance she needed. Nova gripped his face and guided his mouth back to hers.

Kane lifted her off the ground and used the tree to support her as he drew his body to hers. The brush of his arousal along her inner thigh caused her to stiffen. When he pulled his lips away and looked at her, there seemed to be so much he wanted to say.

Instead of speaking, he entered her slowly. Nova closed her eyes as she focused on that connection. Her head fell back, and she moaned.

Kane kept her lifted as they made love against the tree. She braced her hands on his shoulders. The bark scratched lightly through the tunic material as it snagged along her back. She didn't care.

Her greedy body did not let the moment last as long as she wanted it to. Climax took over. She dipped her head forward and bit into his shoulder to keep from crying out as pleasure filled her. She trembled uncontrollably. Almost instantly, Kane joined her in release. He pressed tight against her.

Ragged breathing sounded between them. Nova lifted her head from his shoulder. She felt his chest rising and falling against her breasts. With each pant of air, reality inched its way closer. Kane felt it too. She saw it in his eyes.

He lowered her slowly to the ground. She ignored the sting on her back from rubbing against the tree.

"We can't do this," Nova whispered, not wanting to let him go.

"I think it might be too late for that." He looked as if he wanted to kiss her again.

Nova resisted the urge to stay in his embrace. She leaned over to pull up her pants. The gesture forced him to step back and do the same.

The full force of their actions rushed over her and made it impossible to enjoy the aftermath, even as her heart continued to beat in noticeably fast thumps. She glanced up and down the path. Thankfully it was empty.

"Talk to me," he urged. "What are you thinking?"

"My people will accuse me of betraying them if I go back and tell them medical booths and food simulators aren't harmful." She studied his face. It would be so easy to fall back into his arms. "And if they know about..."

Nova couldn't say it.

"Me?" Kane looked hurt.

Nova nodded. "They'll treat me like they treat Justina. No one takes her seriously. They won't listen. I can't help them if they don't respect me."

Nova felt tears brimming in her eyes. She wiped them before they could fall.

"I understand." Kane sounded deflated. "It is

not my intention to make things more difficult for you."

"If things..." Nova didn't know how to say what she felt. She didn't discuss her emotions. She did what needed to be done. But she couldn't leave things unsaid between them. "If I could..."

"It's all right, Nova. I understand." Kane touched her arm briefly and nodded. The kindness in his eyes made it worse.

"If I had been born with wings, I think I would fly to you too," she managed, "but Cysgodians aren't allowed to have dreams. We belong on the ground."

There was nothing else they could say.

Nova nodded once and turned to leave. Somehow her legs managed to carry her down the path. The feel of his body lingered on her skin, her lips, deep inside. She tasted him in her mouth. Every ounce of her wanted to turn around and look at him, but if she did, she knew she'd never make it all the way down to Shelter City.

13

Nova gasped in surprise as the door to her home opened before she could touch the handle.

Celestial grabbed her arm and jerked her inside to where a small gathering waited. "What did they do to you?"

Nova looked around in surprise to find a half-dozen Revolutionist members in her house. Celestial shut the door. The dim light made it harder to see after being in the sunlight.

"How did you all get into my home?" Nova asked.

"I let them in," Tanja said, standing up from a mat in the corner. The girl stared at her, worried. "I couldn't find you after I saw that shifter take you."

"We were coming up with a plan to rescue you,"

Badar, the only man in the group, said. A childhood accident had left him with a severe limp, and he leaned on his wife, Juno, for support.

"Once we knew where to rescue you from." Juno wore trinkets around her neck that she'd collected from around the city. Nova had been to their home once, and the entire space had been filled with random bits of junk, leaving only tiny paths to walk through and a small space to sleep. Juno wasn't the only person in Shelter City to do that. Some people who had nothing seemed to need to acquire everything they could.

Nova was the opposite. She saw no reason to have things that other people could take away from her. Her home was mostly empty except for a few items that had belonged to her parents and a sleeping mat.

Nova's eyes started to adjust. Narrow light streams came from outside, illuminating the space enough to make out their faces. Each one had taken an active role in the Revolutionists without Nova having to ask.

Mensa stood next to Celestial. The two could often be found together. They spent time trying to talk to and recruit the younger population, those who did not remember the old world. Youth didn't always value the old ways.

Badar and his wife acted as the communications center, even though no one had appointed them to the position. If she wanted to know anything the group was doing or thinking, those two were in the middle of it.

Liberation, better known as Lib, had been born to revolt. Her father had named her that in hopes she'd help him lead the rebellion. Unfortunately, his rebellion had amounted to getting drunk and yelling obscenities up at the facility before peeing on the side of the cliff and passing out. Lib tried to live up to her name but had begun to suffer from the same affliction as her father. She covered it well most of the time, but Nova saw her swaying back and forth as she stood and could smell the trace of alcohol coming from her direction.

"Did they hurt you?" Tonya asked.

Nova shook her head. "They had questions. We just talked."

"The other faction leaders weren't taken," Badar insisted.

"Because they're not seen as a threat," Mensa answered as if it should have been obvious. "We're the strongest."

That wasn't necessarily true. Nova had seen Doyen's crowd on the recording.

Nova crossed to a board affixed to the wall and slid the bottom counterclockwise to expose a small hole and let in more light.

Tanja gasped.

"What happened to your back?" Lib demanded. "Did they beat you?"

Nova tried to reach behind her to feel what they were talking about. Her skin stung a little, but all she felt was material. "It's nothing. I slid down a tree."

It was halfway true.

Their expressions said they didn't believe her.

"We have things to discuss." Nova hoped to get their attention off her back. She hadn't decided how much to tell them, which felt strange because holding back vital information about the health of their people felt like lying.

"Did they name Justina queen?" Badar teased.

"What self-respecting Cysgodian woman would allow herself to be touched by a shifter?" Juno gave a shiver of disgust. "Let alone marry one? It's a mockery."

Badar patted his wife on her shoulder.

Nova forced her eyes to remain lifted as she hid her emotions. "It has been shown to me that our presumptions about the food simulators and medical booths may not be correct."

Silence met her words.

Nova watched them for a response.

After a moment, Badar asked, "In what way? Are they more harmful? I always suspected those things were worse than we imagined."

Juno nodded as if that conjecture made sense to her.

Nova shook her head in denial. "Less."

"Less what?" Lib asked, frowning.

"Less harmful." Nova knew this conversation wasn't going to be met with enthusiasm. "Actually, not harmful. Perfectly safe."

Badar started to laugh, prompting Mensa and Celestial to join him.

"They tried to convince you of that?" Celestial chuckled. "I hope you told them we may be poor, but we are not space cadets."

When Nova didn't join in, their laughter tittered to a stop.

"You can't say you believe them?" Celestial demanded. She leaned closer, searching Nova's eyes. "What did they do to you in there? Uploads? Torture? Injections? Did they erase your thoughts?"

Nova thought of being questioned by Salena, of

confessing things she'd never say out loud. She tried to block the memory of Kane, but the memory of him sent a shiver over her body. She felt colder without him, as if her skin had literally had a layer ripped off when she walked away from him.

"We talked," Nova said. "I have reason to believe they may be telling the truth about food simulators and medical booths. It's not difficult to imagine the Federation was lying to us when they presented the information about the radiation. We know they lied to us about other things. They over-promised our future when rescuing us from Cysgod. This is not the life we were meant to lead. Maybe they lied about radiation triggering a relapse as well."

"Nova, you're our leader, and we respect you, but..." Mensa looked at Celestial in question.

"Their scientists did the most research on the virus," Celestial added.

"However, they do know our fears," Lib reasoned. "It wouldn't have been hard to fake evidence."

"No, Lib," Badar denied. "We saw what happened to those who ate the simulator food that had been smuggled into the city—the shaking, the sickness, the personality changes. Softhearted Ceres never hurt anyone his entire life. He used to help entertain the young ones and taught them things about our history. Then one day, he told me about getting blue bread from a simulator. He wanted me to help smuggle it in so we could give it to the children. He meant well, but not a day later I found him yelling in the street like a madman, chasing two young boys around with a knife. Two days later, I heard they found his body in a back alley. He'd been beaten to death. No one knows who did it."

"How do they explain that?" Juno demanded, always in support of whatever her husband said.

"The Federation drugged him with something that is supposed to cause aggression," Nova explained.

"Why would they do that?" Badar asked, shaking his head. "It would only make more work for their soldiers."

"Yeah, why?" Juno inserted.

"To have an excuse to beat us," Lib answered. "To make us turn on each other for their sport. To test new medicines on us. I can think of many reasons."

The others listened, but because it came from Lib, they were less inclined to take her ideas seriously.

"Did Ceres get the bread from Yellow Shirt?" Nova noticed dust particles floating through the stream of light coming in from the hole. She followed them with her eyes, imagining they were hundreds of tiny dragons flying through the air. "He stole a simulator from the shifters and tainted the food for the Federation."

"Do you have proof of this?" Mensa crossed her arms over her chest. "Yellow Shirt hasn't been seen since the rebellion. He's not around to answer that accusation."

Nova forced thoughts of dragons out of her mind.

"Yellow Shirt would deny any wrongdoing, especially if he did it," Celestial said. "Though his wares normally extended to the lower half of a pleasure droid and refurbished gadgets."

"True." Mensa nodded. "Still makes it hard to prove."

"I heard rumors Yellow Shirt had a unit." Badar looked at his wife, who nodded in confirmation. His words didn't sound confident, but he also wasn't the type to admit he was out of the loop in a conversation.

"None of them can be trusted," Mensa decided.

"What evidence did the shifters show you of the drug or Yellow Shirt?"

"It's difficult to explain. They have a way of forcing the truth. I think we need to stay open to the idea that we might be wrong about the radiation. I'm not asking anyone to dine on simulator food until we can prove that it's safe." Nova knew they'd keep asking for more details about her meeting if she kept talking about it. In an attempt to act as a leader should, she changed the subject. "We have a more pressing matter within the city. I saw a recording of Doyen. He's preaching blood magic again, and his crowd is getting bigger."

"I've heard the same thing," Badar interjected.

"Some of ours were in the gathering," Nova continued. "We need to reach out to them and make sure they know their loyalty is expected."

"Who?" Mensa and Celestial demanded in unison.

"Sagitta and some others from the south district. Also, the one-eyed boy with the black hair, and those two he's always with." Nova frowned. "I would hate to see them fall in with the Blood Fanatics."

Mensa and Celestial shared a look.

"I know where those boys like to hide out," Celestial said. "We'll go talk to them."

Mensa nodded in agreement.

"Good," Nova said. "Report back with what you learn."

"Sagitta owes me a favor," Lib put forth. "Stupid girl. I'll go talk to her and see where her mind is at. I didn't know they were letting women into those Blood Fanatic meetings now. It's about as smart as walking into a fire and expecting it not to burn."

"Remind her of that, Lib." Nova turned to Badar and Juno. "I need you on the street talking to people. See what you can learn about Yellow Shirt and the simulators or the drugs. Find out if the people who became sick had contact with him as the food source."

Nova knew it would be better if they discovered the truth of the drug for themselves. They weren't inclined to believe information that came from the shifters.

"What about me?" Tanja asked.

"I want you to stay here," Nova said. "The Shopkeepers stole the rations for the southern distribution sector. We need to go over the city maps to locate where Gethin might have hidden them."

"I'll see what I can find out about it," Badar interrupted. "Come, Juno."

He led his wife out of the home. The others followed him.

When they were alone, Tanja pulled the door shut tight and asked, "What really happened?"

"Princess Salena of the dragons has a strange gift. Anything she asks must be answered." Nova trusted Tanja not to gossip. "When they were done ensuring I had no plans to harm them, they used her power on one of the princes. He told me about the radiation. I believe him."

"You can't..." Tanja shook her head, tripping over her words. "No. If you say they merely told you and you believed them, it sounds as if they tricked you. You can't tell the others that is how you got the information. They will replace you as the faction leader. Badar wants the role. Don't give him an excuse to take it. You need to show them something they can see."

"You said you saw us?" Nova asked. "Was this after we met last time?"

Tanja hesitated before touching Nova's arm. Tears brimmed her eyes. "I saw him take you. He was with that other one. The woman. I've seen her in the city before, like before the rebellion. I couldn't reach you before you disappeared. Did he...?"

Nova quickly shook her head, understanding the

girl's worry. "He didn't *take* me like that. He brought me to a hidden monitoring station within the city."

"But your back," Tanja insisted.

"It's not what you think. I promise." Nova pulled the girl into a hug. "He never hurt me."

Tanja stiffened at the contact and awkwardly returned the embrace before pulling away.

"I need you to show me where I was when I disappeared." Nova went to the board and slid it over the hole to shut out the light. She went to her sleeping mat and pushed it aside to reveal a small hole she'd dug beneath it to hide an old cloth bag. Pulling it out, she clutched it in her hand and said, "I might have a plan."

14

THE NUMBNESS WOULDN'T LEAVE HIM.

Kane had watched Nova walk away from him. She hadn't looked back, and he couldn't look away. Even when she disappeared into the city, he'd stared after her. It was only when Roderic and Justina found him that he'd had no choice but to force his mind from thoughts of her.

That was a lie. His thoughts were still on her.

"If I had been born with wings, I think I would fly to you too, but Cysgodians aren't allowed to have dreams. We belong on the ground."

In some ways, it would have been better if she'd said nothing. Those words echoed in his mind, giving him hope in a hopeless situation. He could no more ask her to choose him over her people than he could abandon his own responsibilities.

Maybe someday.

He would wait for her.

He would wait forever.

If they weren't mated, she wouldn't have forever. He couldn't share his long life with her. She was Cysgodian. He would live hundreds of years without her.

The thought left him cold.

Roderic sat on the ground next to him as they overlooked the city. Their legs dangled over the side of the cliff. Out of all the shifters, Roderic understood most of what Kane was up against since he had married a Cysgodian woman.

"Does Justina miss living in the city?" Kane glanced at his friend. "I know her people have had a hard time adjusting to her new role."

Roderic turned to look down at the barracks where his wife had gone. Aside from a couple of Var guards walking the area, the barracks' yard was empty. Justina helped organize the expected influx of new residents from the city. "Fiora predicted that they will come around and accept her."

"Still, it can't be easy."

"No," Roderic agreed. "I know their rejection

hurts her. Like when we met with the faction leaders. I wanted to crawl over that table and shake each
one of them." He cleared his throat. "I didn't mean
to threaten Nova."

Kane gestured in slight dismissal. "You don't
have to apologize for defending your wife. These
meetings have been tense for everyone. We are
fortunate to have Justina on our side. And the
Cysgodians are lucky to have her even if they don't
realize it yet. History will remember that she was the
catalyst that saved them from the Federation."

Roderic nodded. "And you might not see the
path forward, but that does not mean it's not there."

The forest was at their backs, giving privacy to
the conversation. The sound of small animals moved
in the trees behind them, rustling leaves. It
contrasted with the busy flow of people below. An
occasional shout drifted up, backdropped by the low
murmur of a crowd.

"There were so many times I didn't see a way
forward with Justina," Roderic said. "Our love could
have ruined the treaty with the Federation and
compromised shifter survival. Instead, it led to
events that have freed Shelter City."

Kane appreciated what Roderic was trying to
say, but it gave him little comfort. "You and your

wife were on the same side. The Cysgodians now see us as the enemy. To them, we have taken the place of the Federation. Her people will not accept me, and I can't ask her to betray them to be with me. It took us thirty years to get to this point."

Roderic took a deep breath and held it. After a long moment, he said, "Perhaps you both should leave Qurilixen. Find a new home in space or travel the deep black with the others. No one cares up there. Negotiations will go on without you. Give up life here to be together. Then, perhaps, in time, you can return. What are thirty years compared to hundreds?"

It wasn't the solution Kane wanted. Duty and desire warred within him. What kind of example would he be to his people if he took off to space right now?

Could he give up everything to gain the one thing he really wanted?

Yes, if Nova asked him. He would go without hesitance.

Could he ask her to leave her people behind?

"No," Kane answered Roderic. "Nova lost her homeworld once. I will not ask her to do it again. The best I can hope for is to end this mounting conflict before it explodes, prove to the Cysgodians we are not the enemy, get the factions to come to an understanding..."

Kane frowned as more items came to his mental list.

"Stop Doyen from trying to consume shifters, keep the Federation from returning and starting a war, prepare for the Lithorian negotiations that were postponed due to their ship trouble, or have every Draig woman mad at me—"

"Don't let fear take over. I hardly think chocolate shipments will affect the outcome of your future." Roderic patted Kane on the back.

"Then you haven't met Draig women. They insist on it for the mating ceremony." Kane knew he wasn't being completely reasonable. "If someday Nova agrees to go to the ceremony with me, I want her to have everything."

Something rustled in the trees behind them. Kane ignored the animals. His attention remained focused on the city. There were many people, but he still found himself concentrating on the crowd trying to find her.

"It's strange to think she's been down there all these years. I've flown over this city so many times. But she's been here the entire time. I've probably glanced over her head, and she's looked at the sky to see me." Kane took a deep breath. It was not the first time the idea crossed his mind, but it was the first he'd said it out loud. "My crystal never glowed. Maybe the gods knew we would not be together, and they were trying to spare us the pain of it."

He kept searching through the sea of faces for hers as if seeing her now would be a sign for the future.

"And maybe the gods knew it was too soon," Roderic countered. He glanced behind them into the trees. Several small animals ran through the underbrush. When the noise settled, he turned back to the city. "There is much to be said about tradition, and it pleases the elders when we follow the old ways, but you don't need crystals and mating ceremonies. In the end, all you need is the will of two people to make it so. I have only known gods to point out a path. It is up to us to figure out how to cross over it. Don't let a rock dictate what you were born to know."

As a cat-shifter, Roderic couldn't understand how much faith the dragons put into that rock. The crystal was as part of Kane as shifting or breathing fire. The glow wasn't a trick. It was a beacon calling out for something the animal inside couldn't verbalize—the need for his mate. His entire life he'd put confidence into its power to predict his happiness.

"You are right. I must have patience," Kane said.

"That's not what I said. I think you have to fight," Roderic corrected. "Fight for her, for your happiness, for your people, her people, everything. Show those gods you're not backing—"

Roderic's words stopped with a small gasp. The cat-shifter's eyes rounded and glazed over before he crumpled forward.

Kane half-shifted as he grabbed Roderic's wrist, catching him before his friend slid down the cliff. Two metal darts stuck out of the man's arm and a third from his neck. A fourth dart whizzed past them.

Kane quickly jerked the cat-shifter back over the side onto the ground. He crouched over Roderic, protecting him as he scanned the forest, and pulled the darts from his body.

The small animals had gone silent. If he hadn't been so preoccupied with Nova, he would have detected the change.

Another dart flew toward his face, and he batted it away. Kane tracked its origin into the trees. He roared to alert the Var guards at the facility as he took off after the shooter.

Movement converged on him from both sides. Kane acted on instinct, blocking the attacks. His fist met solid flesh as he kicked one way and then punched another. Someone tried to grab him from behind, and he spun to the side, lifting his arms to break the hold and send the man flying into a thick tree trunk.

The attackers wore hoods and jumped out from behind trees. Their scent had been poorly obscured by dirt as he detected the sting of moonshine on the air. A low whistle resonated in the forest. The sound of running feet came from the distance to form a second wave of attack. Kane changed course, retreating toward Roderic.

Two men had a net wrapped around Roderic's body. Kane tried to roar again, but a wave of dizziness caused him to stumble. He fell to his knees. Darts stuck into his thigh and stomach. He swatted at them to get them out, but his coordination was off. He crawled to stop them from taking Roderic. Three sharp stings hit his back, piercing his dragon armor.

Kane collapsed onto his stomach. Fallen leaves cushioned the fall. He grabbed a handful, trying to use them as leverage to drag himself forward.

"Go down," a man commanded. Two more darts stung his back.

Boots blocked Kane's view of Roderic being taken.

"Leave the guards. They're too close to the facility. We don't need them." The voice came as if from far away. "Get these two while the others are still inside."

Kane tried to focus his hearing even as his vision darkened. He tried to roar, swiping at the nearby foot. His taloned hand hit an ankle and, as the poison took complete hold, he had the grim satisfaction of hearing the crack of the man's fall.

15

"WHAT ARE WE LOOKING FOR?" TANJA ASKED, rushing to stay close to Nova.

"A secret alley." Nova moved down the street. Every place in Shelter City was familiar, but she now looked for something easy to miss. She'd tucked the cloth bag into her waistband to hide it under her shirt.

"There's nothing down this way but storage," Tanja said. "Old salvage engine parts from the ship that were no good for building and need fuel cells to work."

Nova moved along the street, focusing her attention on the right. Kane had turned in that direction before going into the tight space. Most of the narrow spaces between buildings were wide enough to pass between. Footprints had worn a path over the ground in most of them.

Not many people bothered with this part of the city, but there were still a few who passed through on their way to other places. Loud clanging sounded as a group of teenagers threw rocks at a building. Tanja grabbed Nova's arm and used her body as a shield to hide from the boys as they passed.

"Problem?" Nova asked.

"Suitor," Tanja responded. "Some of the boys decided they would pick wives and made a pact to stay away from each other's futures. I'd rather throw myself from the tower than partner with Vace."

"That's disgusting." Nova frowned.

"Eh." Tanja shrugged. "Keeps the others at bay for the most part. Just because he wants me doesn't mean he'll get me."

"You should not have to be so wise," Nova said, more to herself.

"How is that wise?" Tanja again put space between them.

"I simply wish you had more time for childhood." Nova slowed down as the spaces between buildings narrowed significantly. She stopped to peer down a shaded alleyway. Seeing a definite end, she continued.

Tanja gave a small laugh. "That doesn't make sense. I have as much time as anyone."

Nova went to the next crevice and peered between two metal structures. "This might be the one. It's the right width, and I remember this texture on the metal."

Tanja dipped under Nova's arm to look for herself. "There's nothing down there."

"Make sure no one is looking. I'm going in." Nova glanced around before slipping sideways through the opening. She closed her eyes like the first time she'd journeyed down the secret path. It felt the same.

She heard a rustling next to her and opened her eyes. Tanja had joined her.

"I'm coming too," Tanja whispered. "What's in here? What are we looking for?"

"A cyborg with answers."

The sound of footsteps thundered past as shouts came from the pack of boys. None of them turned to look down the narrow alleyway.

Nova kept moving, this time watching as she felt her way along. Her hands found a corner, and she moved under the shade of a metal roof into darkness.

"Are you sure?" Tanja asked, staying on the edge

of the dim light. "I haven't seen any of the sweeper borgs active since the rebellion."

"He's not a sweeper. This is the way," Nova assured her. "Don't be afraid. There's nothing in the dark."

Tanja's breath sounded abnormally heavy, and she hesitated before following Nova. "Don't leave me."

Nova felt around for the girl's hand and clasped it tightly. They turned another corner. "We should be almost there."

Nova's foot hit a step, and she gasped in surprise.

"What happened?" Tanja demanded.

Nova had forgotten about that part. Her toe throbbed. "I'm going to let go and look for the entrance. Be careful. There's a step."

Tanja's feet slid in the dirt as she inched after Nova.

Nova felt around the wall, turning as she looked for any seam that she could pry apart to let them into Yevgen's den.

"Be careful in here," Nova warned. "I don't think he'll hurt us, but if I tell you to run, don't hesitate. Just get out of there."

Nova found the edge of a board and pushed it

open slowly. Blue glowed from inside the cyborg's home. Tanja gasped, and Nova saw the girl's shocked expression.

"Hello, Yev—"

A loud blast from a pistol cut off her words as it fired in the small space.

"Nova!" Tanja tried to pull her arm.

"Back away," Yevgen warned. "I will protect myself."

"It's Nova," she tried to explain through the cracked door. "From earlier."

"I know who it is," Yevgen answered. "This isn't a stop on the planetary home tour circuit. Turn around, or I'll make sure every second of your life is broadcast to the rest of the city."

As far as a threat went, it was a good one. Nova wasn't sure if he could do it or not but seeing his previous surveillance, she was inclined to believe him.

"I have a trade to make." Nova pulled the bag from her waistband and slowly lifted her hand through the doorway. "In this bag."

She waited, and no answer came.

"Yevgen?" Nova asked.

"Enter."

Nova opened the door all the way and peeked

inside. The smell from the blaster discharge scented the air. Yevgen sat at his wall of monitors. They flashed through cityscapes. He placed the blaster pistol on the console.

"I have someone with me. May she enter?" Nova asked, keeping her eyes on the pistol in case he tried to go for it again.

"Don't touch anything, Tanja," Yevgen said, revealing he already knew who was with her. His screens brought up images of Tanja from around the city—jumping over a wall, curled into a small ball behind an old ship engine, arguing with another girl, with Nova before the soldier Mure appeared outside the ration distribution facility, and finally punching Vace when he tried to kiss her. Since the scenes looped, Vace was hit repeatedly.

Good, Nova thought before turning to wave the girl inside. "Tanja."

"*How—?* Why is that up there?" Tanja demanded.

Nova gave a slight shake of her head and didn't answer as she gestured for Tanja to stay close to the door.

The cyborg's eyes focused on Nova's hand. "What's in the bag?"

"You like information." Nova's answer was more of a statement than a question.

Yevgen nodded. Alien symbols replaced the onscreen images. Nova couldn't begin to read them.

"I want to make a trade."

Again, he nodded, his eyes staying on the bag. The robotic irises whirled, and an image of the bag appeared behind him. Dimension lines outlined her hand as if he measured to guess what might be inside.

"I have something you've never seen." She gave the bag a tiny shake. "A newspaper chip from Cysgod from when the virus started. My father had a subscription, so it would have loaded everything the paper put out before the end. He had it in his pocket when we took him to the hospital. They handed it to me and, somehow, I still had it when we arrived here. It's all I have of his. I thought maybe you could read it and make a copy."

Yevgen reached out his hand. The screens went black, darkening the room. A blurry photo of a small planet appeared in the center. "I have no good Cysgod images on file. Only this planetary survey from the Federation archives."

Nova pulled the bag back. "You're working with the Federation?"

That was not the impression she'd gotten when Kane brought her here.

His eyes flashed with red briefly. "I accessed their databases through an unsecured data portal."

"I'll need information in return," Nova stated, still not giving the chip to him.

"That is why people usually come here to trade," Yevgen answered, sounding unamused.

"And I need full recordings. None of that chopped-up mess you showed the shifters about me. That wasn't the full conversation you recorded, and you know it." Nova came deeper into the home.

"What are you talking about?" Tanja tried to whisper, but the sound carried easily.

Yevgen lowered his hand. "The extra drones deployed in battle scrambled transmissions all over the city. There were many instances to record and sort. Information is still being recovered."

Nova knew she'd made him defensive. This was not the way to make a quick deal. Still, it had needed to be said. She didn't appreciate what he'd implied about her last time. She also couldn't think of any other option than to ask him for what she needed.

"As a faction leader, I need honest, complete proof that the Federation was drugging simulator food to make us believe it was bad for us." Nova glanced at Tanja. "That they distributed it through the vendor Yellow Shirt. I also need any proof that they lied to us about medical booths."

"No." Yevgen's screens flashed through city scenes.

"What do you mean, no?" Nova's eyes strayed to the blaster, but he didn't reach for it. "Don't you want the newspaper chip?"

The measured image of her hand appeared behind him, giving away his thoughts.

"The trade is not acceptable." He turned his back on her and faced the monitors. City scenes reappeared as he searched the streets.

"That's everything," Tanja said, coming to stand beside Nova for a better look. "All of Shelter City."

"Then what trade would be acceptable?" Nova asked. "I can't leave here without the truth."

"You can if I allow it," he stated.

"I didn't mean to offend you. I want to trade. What do you want?" Nova put her hand out, stopping Tanja from going closer. She nodded toward the blaster pistol in case the girl had not seen the weapon.

"I wish for you to leave and never return. You do not have an invitation. If you try to tell anyone where I am, I will share all your secrets. I will share the secrets of Tanja. I will share the secrets of anyone who is kind to you. I will be watching. Leave my home now."

"Please, Yevgen, all I need is the truth." Nova softened her voice like Payton had done with him. "And if that is what you want, I will leave afterward."

"You will leave now," he stated, still watching the city.

Nova tried a different approach. "I understand you can't find what I need. It was a difficult request."

Yevgen stiffened at the challenge.

"Princess Payton made it sound like you were all-powerful, but I get it. The drones are too formidable." Nova gave an audible sigh.

Images of flying drones flashed.

"Those substandard machines—" Yevgen turned to face them. He smiled, though the expression looked more vindictive than pleasant. "You wish for your friend to see your truth?"

Nova frowned and glanced at Tanja.

Every screen filled with a view of Nova and Kane kissing in the alleyway in various stages—gravitating together, lips locked, lips parted, Kane coming down the alley after her.

Seeing it caused a wave of longing to rush

through her and her breath caught. Nova couldn't bring herself to look at Tanja.

Yevgen chuckled. "I keep plenty of secret truths here. Most of them are things people do not want out there in the world. Why should I give you the truth you ask for? What makes you better than the rest?"

Tanja dove forward, hands outreached as she tried to go for the blaster. Before Nova knew what was happening, Tanja fumbled to point the stolen blaster back at the cyborg.

"Do you think I'd leave a live weapon out?" he asked.

Tanja pointed it away from him and pulled the trigger. It clicked several times.

Yevgen drew a pistol and pointed it at Tanja. She instantly dropped the dead blaster on the floor.

Tanja backed up until she hit the wall. She trembled and held her hands to the side.

"We'll leave," Nova said, stretching her arm to the side as she inched to stand in front of the girl to shield her. "We won't come back."

"At this range it will go through both of you." Yevgen brought up images of people being shot by Federation blasters before finally showing Mure.

"We're leaving." Nova reached behind her and

found Tanja's arm. She held tight as she began to walk sideways toward the door.

Yevgen fired.

Nova jolted in surprise. Tanja whimpered in fright. They stopped moving.

"Give me the girl, and I'll let you leave," Yevgen said.

Nova instantly shook her head. "No. I'm not going anywhere without her."

The screens flashed several times, and she automatically glanced at them. An image of Yellow Shirt appeared carrying a food simulator. Next came a picture of him with a Federation soldier with the name *Sever* showing on his uniform.

Yevgen had the information she needed.

"Give me the girl, and I'll give you the proof you seek," Yevgen offered.

Tanja leaned around Nova to look. She held onto Nova's arm. "He has it."

"No," Nova said. "I'll give you the newspaper chip."

"I want the girl." Yevgen brought up a data file that looked like a scientific briefing about the Cysgod virus. "My princess gave me access to the Federation's facility database today. I can find what you want."

"Nova, you have to," Tanja said. "That's every-thing we need to prove the food and medical care is safe."

"No." Nova shook her head.

"You can save Shelter City from starvation and pain," Tanja insisted.

"No."

"I know why you were too ashamed to tell me that you seduced a dragon for information," Tanja said. "I know you did it for all of us. I can...take...a...that thing."

Yevgen scrunched up his face in disgust. "I have no use for your taking. You will be my assistant. I will fit you with bionic parts so that you will process files for me. Your bones are weak. I will replace them with metal."

Tanja's grip tightened.

"I will never trade her." Nova sat the bag on the console. Holding onto the past was not worth sacri-ficing the future. "This in trade for our lives. We're leaving now."

Nova turned and urged Tanja to walk in front of her toward the door. She held her breath, waiting for a blast to strike her in the back.

As her hand reached the wooden door, Yevgen stated, "I accept the original trade. Copy of the chip for the proof you seek. If it is in the database, I will uncover it."

When Tanja stepped through the door to safety, Nova turned back to see Yevgen pulling the newspaper chip out of the bag along with several payment stones. He swept the stones back inside and tossed the bag over his shoulder, keeping only the information. The money landed on the floor near Nova's feet.

"Why?" Nova asked, not trusting the cyborg.

Yevgen paused to give her a matter-of-fact answer. "She shot to the side and did not try to kill me. You took less than a second to think about her fate. She was willing to give herself up for the good of others. You were willing to save her against your best interests."

"So it was a test?" Nova held up her hand to keep Tanja from coming back inside.

"Isn't everything?" Yevgen's screen showed Nova standing behind him. "You are not your brother. He would have given a different answer."

"No, I'm nothing like him." Nova was tired of having to defend herself against the actions of Doyen.

"You and the dragon prince." Yevgen turned on his sling. The casters creaked overhead.

"What about us?" Nova thought about his kiss that had been onscreen moments before.

"Is Tanja correct? Did you seduce him to get what you wanted?"

Nova shook her head. "I won't talk about that."

In truth, she didn't want to think about Kane.

"Answer my—" The cyborg's eyes flashed, and he frowned. He spun back to the console and began typing. Aerial views of the city showed on his screens. Dragons flew through the sky, spreading out over the trees.

"What is it? What's happening?" Nova came up behind him to get a better look. A line of cloaked Blood Fanatics ran through a side street, scattering the small crowd gathered there.

"Was it a lie with the dragon?" Yevgen asked. "That look on your face. Was it a lie? Did you seduce him to get what you wanted?"

Nova didn't answer.

"I am trying to remember what it was like to have emotions," Yevgen continued. One of the monitors stopped on her face when she was with Kane. The rest followed the runners and logged their identities whenever enough of their faces showed from beneath their hooded cloaks.

Even she couldn't describe her paused expression, but she remembered what she'd felt. Fear. Not of him so much as how he made her feel when he was near.

"Answer him," Tanja urged from the doorway.

Her image flickered and changed to Kane's face. The other screens stuttered and skipped, showing the runners moving backward as Yevgen retraced their steps.

"No. It wasn't a lie or a trick. I tried to resist. He's a shifter. Nothing about our being together makes sense." Nova still felt his hands on her body, his lips on her mouth. It didn't take much for the longing to surge to the surface.

"You love him," Tanja stated. "If it doesn't make sense and you did it anyway, you must love him. Leading the Revolutionists has been your destiny. I have never known you to do anything that wasn't in service to that destiny."

Love?

Nova started to shake her head. "I—"

"They came from the trees," Yevgen interrupted. "They should not have come from the trees. That is too close to the stronghold facility."

"Who?" Tanja asked, returning to the monitors even though Nova waved her to keep back.

"Doyen's men." Yevgen flashed their faces.

Nova had a bad feeling. She watched as the cyborg traced the Blood Fanatics into the forest. The image paused.

"I do not have cameras there," Yevgen said.

A sick feeling built in her stomach.

"What is that?" Nova pointed between trees. In all honesty, the blur looked like a small tree, and she wasn't sure why she pointed at it.

Yevgen zoomed in and sharpened the image. The outline of two men dragging a body came into view.

"Kane," Nova whispered as a desperate feeling washed over her. She had no evidence to back up her claim. From looks alone, the body on the ground could have been any of the dragon men. Yet, something inside her told her she needed to help Kane.

"I can't identify who—" Yevgen fiddled with the image.

"It's Kane." Nova touched the screen where the man dragged him. "Who is this?"

The cyborg swatted her arm. "Don't smudge the viewer."

The image zoomed in on the abductors, but it was impossible to make out their faces.

"See that?" Yevgen nodded toward where her

hand had been. "Tan fur, maybe? They could be Var?"

"That doesn't make sense. Are they rescuing him?" Nova wanted to reach across the console and force the picture to show at a better angle.

Yevgen began to search the tree line to no avail.

"Where are Doyen's men now?" Nova asked.

That search took less time. Yevgen scanned the city and stopped as he found one of the men being let into a building on the edge of the city.

"Are those drag marks on the ground?" Nova leaned forward, almost touching the screen but stopping herself before making contact. A long line traced through the dirt leading to the doorway.

"That is where Doyen speaks to his followers," Tanja said. "You don't want to go there."

"Yevgen, I need your blaster." Nova didn't give him time to refuse as she reached next to his leg to snatch it from him. She urged Tanja back toward the entryway. "We have to go."

"I want that weapon returned when you are finished," Yevgen stated. "And you'll owe me an hour's worth of information in exchange for its use."

"What about the evidence?" Tanja asked. "We can't leave yet."

"I'll come back for it later." Nova ushered the girl into the dark passageway.

"I don't know why you're panicking. He's a dragon. He can take care of himself. Besides, you heard Yevgen. It sounds like the cats have him already. I'm sure he's fine," Tanja said. "You can't go where the Blood Fanatics hang out, even if it sounds like women have started showing up to his speeches. They're idiots to go near that crowd."

Nova couldn't answer or explain. The sick feeling in her stomach only intensified. All she knew was she needed to find Kane.

16

THE STEADY CREAK OF ROPE AGAINST WOOD groaned in time with the sway of Kane's upside-down body. He tried to focus his vision, but he felt lightheaded and nauseous each time he opened his eyes. He concentrated on the sounds and smells instead.

Kane heard the hushed murmur of voices around him and the rhythmic clang of metal on metal that always seemed to ring out over Shelter City like a beacon to tell him where it was from the sky. He smelled the unmistakable scent of the city—rust, sweat, and stale dust. It reminded him of the inside of an old spacecraft that had once landed with dignitaries from another planet. No other place on Qurilixen smelled like this.

The rope tugged at his ankles, hoisting him higher. His bound hands dragged against dirt before finding air. The wood creaked in protest. Dizziness caused his head to swim.

The voices grew louder, and excitement buzzed through the air. He tried to pick apart the conversations, but the words were jumbled.

A thought whispered through his mind, telling him he should shift and fight. His body was unable to obey the command.

More creaks sounded and then a pained moan. The noise called forth the memory of Roderic on the ground. There had been darts. He remembered the sound of them whizzing past. And running feet. They'd thumped and swooshed in the forest litter.

How did the Cysgodians get darts?

How did they navigate the forest undetected?

He had smelled alcohol, the potent nose-stinging stench of moonshine from the stills. Were the Cysgodians trading with the marsh farmers?

As soon as his mind started to track through his thoughts, they blurred into a fog he couldn't fight his way across. Numbness filled each limb until all he had was the impression of bound wrists and ankles. He dipped in and out of darkness, unsure how long it lasted each time.

"I have promised you immortality."

The words jolted Kane from the fog. The sound of a gathering grew louder, a crescendo of noise that pulled him further awake.

"I have told you the path we must take."

Doyen. The man's distinct voice was unmistakable, full of bravado and ego.

"You are the true believers. That is why you will be amongst the first to taste the true power of this planet. It's not the three suns, the blue radiation like they'd have us believe."

Cheers erupted, the sound tainted with anger and frustration.

Kane tried to respond, but only a moan passed his lips. A gag had been strapped around his head, keeping his jaw pried open. His vision remained blurry, but he got the impression of a crowd below where he hung over a raised platform. Doyen paced past his view.

Kane jerked, trying to get his body to respond and shift fully. The movement caused the crowd to laugh. He swung back and forth, rotating slowly.

Through the blur, he caught the impression of Roderic hanging by his feet next to him. His friend's lids hung half-open over his eyes, but he didn't appear to see. A gag covered his mouth.

One of the cloaked Blood Fanatics slid a metal trough beneath the cat-shifter's head. It did not take imagination to figure out what they were doing.

Doyen kept talking, spewing his rhetoric about blood magic. The lies inflamed his followers.

Even as his mind became more aware, Kane's body refused to act. The poison from the darts kept him immobile. He tried to focus on his surroundings, searching for anything that could lead to salvation.

There was nothing. No one.

Roderic jerked and blinked, indicating he too was becoming aware.

They needed time for their bodies to fight the poison, to gain control of their movements, to stop this insanity. Kane tried to speak, but the gag kept his weak voice muffled.

The cloaked man slid a second trough underneath him. The action stirred dust particles into the air. They danced around Kane's head, drifting into his nose.

"I would never ask you to do what I haven't done myself. I have tasted the—"

Kane sneezed. The sound stopped Doyen mid-speech.

"I've seen the power," another follower declared

into the pause. "Our leader had been cut, buried, blood streaming down his side. It was enough to kill any man here within seconds, though perhaps in minutes for one as big as you, Giant."

The followers laughed.

"But he crawled out of the grave they left him in and by the next morning, he had completely healed! I witnessed it with my own eyes." The man finished.

"I healed with the power of blood magic!" Doyen announced, taking the attention back.

Kane wanted to yell that it was all a lie. The only way the man could have survived is if he had gotten access to a handheld medic. Panic threaded through him. Roderic had stopped moving, and his eyes were closed. Kane did not want to watch his friend die. This couldn't be their end. Not like this. Not here. Not as a prop to support a madman's trickery.

"You must believe in the power," Doyen continued. "Take it in and let it flow through you."

Kane's mind moved as if in a dream. He thought of Nova and wanted desperately to fight his way back to her. He should have stopped her from walking down that path. He should have told her that if Cysgodians had to remain on the ground, then he'd never fly again. He could have admitted his only dream was to be with her. He would resign his position and live in Shelter City if that is what she needed from him.

Or he would move into the watchtower so he could keep an eye and wait.

Wait until she was ready.

Or he would take her away from here. Into space.

Or he would work to ensure the Cysgodians knew the truth. Whatever she wanted.

None of this could be done hanging upside-down over a trough.

He willed his limbs to shift but only managed to feel a tingling in one of his fingers. Helplessness filled him. His dragon stayed asleep. To his hazy recollection, he had never been stuck in human form.

A loud grunt sounded, followed by the smell of blood. The scent brought Kane back to the present, and he opened his eyes to see the crowd. They focused their attention away from him and began chanting in excitement.

"Blood! Blood! Blood..."

Roderic!

Kane used all the strength he could muster to try

to wiggle his way around toward Roderic. He swung and rotated.

Several men wore dark robes, some so tattered with holes they revealed the clothing beneath. They crowded forward, bowls and cups in both hands like they were about to offer them to the gods.

"Blood is—"

A blast cut off Doyen's words, and sparks exploded on the metal roof of the building. They rained down over the crowd. The men darted for cover as confusion set in.

"Get back." Nova's voice sounded far away. "Doyen, order them to let me pass, or I start shooting!"

"Let her through," Doyen answered. "The leader of the Revolutionist faction is always welcome here."

Kane wished he could see what was happening. His body had rotated toward a rusted wall and put the crowd at his back. He tried to pick out the sound of Nova's steps under the shuffle of feet. He wanted to yell at her to get out of the building.

"To what do we owe this visit?" Doyen asked.

"We need to talk." Nova sounded closer.

"The weapon is unnecessary." Doyen paced across the platform toward Roderic. He didn't appear concerned. "If you wanted a meeting with me, all you had to do was ask. But now is not a good time. We're in the middle of something if you couldn't tell."

"Tell them to leave us."

"I can't do that," Doyen denied.

Roderic didn't make a sound, but the smell of blood remained.

"Doyen, you need to let them go," Nova ordered. "You know they're princes. They will be missed. Their families will come looking."

The crowd began to cheer with various shouts for royal blood. Kane rotated around to see the cloaked figures pressed to one side of the room.

"Quiet!" Nova yelled.

The sound of the blaster shot into the air, and more sparks rained down.

Kane wished his body would rotate farther so he could look at her. What was she thinking coming in here alone?

"Killing members of the royal shifter families will bring harm down on us all. There is no one to help us fight this time." Nova lifted her voice as she spoke to the crowd. "The dragons can set this entire town on fire."

"And we will rise from the ashes," Doyen boasted. "Immortal!"

"Who here wants to face the cat's claw?" Nova tried to speak reason, but this was Doyen's loyal group, and they only responded to his bravado. "Can you rise from a severed throat?"

"I was cut, and I healed," Doyen dismissed.

"Not to mention the Federation is likely on its way back here to demand answers about the rebellion. Do you think we can face them on our own?"

"Let them come!" Doyen yelled. "Those loyal to me will be gone from the city by the time they arrive."

"We need the shifters on our side," Nova insisted. "Hiding in the forest isn't an answer. The land doesn't belong to us. We can't just invade their territory."

"These royals have less control over their population than you give them credit for," Doyen said. "Shifters are on our side. Just not *these* shifters. Have I ever lied to you? I told you the Federation would fall by my hand, and they have fallen. I moved the pieces to bring them down. Me! I stood up to the shifters when they tried to set up rule over us. I told them no! Not today! Not ever! And I told you I would find us a proper sacrifice to cure the virus once and for all and give us eternal life. And here they are. One cat. One dragon. Pure royal blood."

Chants again lifted over the room, drowning out any attempt Nova might make to speak reason and dispute her brother's lies.

"Blood! Blood! Blood..."

17

"Blood! Blood..."

Nova tried to keep her hand steady as she pointed the blaster in her brother's direction. She knew coming into this building was akin to stepping into a poisonous givre nest. All these followers would attack without question if Doyen gave the order. But she also believed, in the end, her brother wouldn't hurt her. They were family. That had to stand for something. And, as much as she tried to deny it, that connection meant something to her. Salena had forced her to face as much.

"You do not need to fear, Nova. No one here will hurt you," Doyen said, the loud words clearly not just for her benefit. Her brother always liked an audience and a chance to show off his power over others. "Come. Drink with me. Join us in immortality."

Nova tried to keep her eyes from lingering on Kane. If she looked at him too long, Doyen would notice. Metal darts stuck into his body in various locations. She didn't see any blood coming from him, but Roderic had a gash down his arm, and his blood dripped into a long pan below. She willed both princes to shift. Surely, they could free themselves if they transformed into animals.

Nova lowered her voice and stepped toward her brother. "You can't really believe that drinking blood will give you immortality or power."

Doyen glanced down at the knife he carried.

"I made it up, Doyen." Nova lowered her weapon to her side, hoping he would do the same. She spoke softly, not wanting to be overheard and knowing that his followers watched intently. She touched his arm. "It was just a stupid story I told you as a boy. You were so scared. There is no blood magic. It can't cure us or give us magical powers. You have to let this idea go. If you truly want to lead our people, then lead them to the truth, *with* the truth. You have a chance to do real good, be a real leader."

"Truth, *sister*?" Doyen answered loudly as if his

words would embarrass her. "Are we admitting the truth now?"

Nova glanced away. Their connection wasn't a secret as much as a forgotten fact.

Doyen lifted his knife higher.

"Don't." Nova glanced at Kane.

Their word. *Don't.*

Doyen looked at Kane and then back to his sister. He pointed his blade at the dragon prince before directing it back to Nova. He waved it between them.

"I thought it was strange the way you looked at him in the meeting." Doyen moved toward Kane. His lips curled in disgust. "You know I would never allow such a pairing."

She didn't need his permission.

Nova lifted the blaster. "Don't."

"And you dare to lecture me about how I choose to lead our people? When you have secrets with this animal?" Doyen jerked Kane's leg, forcing him to spin around to face her.

"Doyen, don't," Nova begged. Kane's eyes were open, and he looked at her, but he didn't move. His chest lifted with shallow breaths. His fingers flexed, but his arms didn't stray from where they hung. She couldn't shoot her brother. She wished someone would come bursting through the door to help her stop this.

Doyen lifted the knife. "Hand my sister a cup. She's going to join us."

"She is a woman," a cloaked member said in surprise. "Subservient."

"You will obey me, or you will not drink!" Doyen shouted at the naysayer who dared question his decree. The large man they called Giant strode a couple of steps and punched the man who had talked. The crowd parted and let their fellow member fall. He didn't move. Giant crossed his arms, and the others quieted.

Her wish for help was not granted.

Nova lifted the blaster and tried to sound confident. "Let him down, my brother. End this."

"You're not going to shoot me." Doyen grinned. His eyes lit with a challenge. She knew that expression. This was a game to him, and he didn't think he could lose. "Where's the loyalty in that? How would the Revolutionists feel about you choosing the life of a shifter over a fellow Cysgodian? What would our father say about you shooting your brother after he told you to watch out for me? What would our mother say if she knew you were trying to grab all the power for yourself instead of helping me to my rightful place? Such arrogance doesn't suit you, Nova."

"Don't bring our parents into this." Nova felt anger bubbling that he'd dare to manipulate her with the past. They'd been children. Yes, she stepped into her inherited role. Yes, he believed he was meant to rule over them. "Their ambitions for us on a dead planet are not our destinies on this one."

"Shoot him. You can't kill him." One of the Blood Fanatics sat a cup on the raised platform and slid it toward Nova's feet. "He's immortal."

Doyen's expression faltered by small degrees as others in his flock shouted their agreement.

"Shoot him! Shoot him! Blood! Blood!"

"This is just the beginning," Doyen said, softer than before.

His followers quieted and inched closer. She heard their feet shuffling and glanced between them and her brother.

"Join me, Nova." Doyen wasn't listening to reason. "Let's do it together just as we were destined on Cysgod. Stand behind me as I lead our people into the future."

She met Kane's eyes. The sound of dripping blood came from Roderic. Why weren't they shifting? One breath of fire would end all of this. One claw could cut them down.

"Not this future." Nova shook her head. She steadied her aim. She didn't want to shoot anyone, even if her brother deserved it.

Doyen gazed over his followers and lifted his knife. Nova took the moment he was distracted by his followers' admiration to charge at him, intent on knocking the weapon from him.

She'd severely miscalculated. Doyen was too strong. He swung his arm, deflecting her with a sweep to her neck and a knee to her stomach. The blaster fell from her hand on impact. Nova dropped to the platform. She cradled her stomach as she looked up at her brother.

He smiled at her, a cruel, bitter look as he again lifted his knife.

"Blood," a man yelled.

"Blood," another answered him.

"Blood. Blood. Blood," they started chanting.

No matter how hard she willed it, Nova knew she couldn't make Doyen change course with mere words. She scurried for the weapon she'd dropped.

Doyen faced Kane. Nova fumbled to pick up the blaster as she rolled on the floor. "Doyen, stop!"

Doyen stabbed downward.

Kane grunted.

Nova fired.

The blast stopped the chanting in a collective gasp.

Time felt as if it slowed. Doyen gripped the knife as he turned to look at her in surprise. Nova kept the blaster raised. Her hand trembled violently, and it was all she could do to hold on. Her brother took two exaggerated breaths before his hand opened, and the blade dropped to the platform. The knife clanged on the floor.

Doyen reached behind his back before bringing bloody fingers up to his face. He fell to his knees.

Nova crawled toward them before struggling to her feet. She made a wide arc around her brother. Doyen lifted his hand. His shocked eyes followed her. She pointed the blaster at the crowd, but they stood transfixed, not moving, as if watching a performance.

Blood ran down from a cut on Kane's arm and dripped into the trough. Nova pulled the darts out of his body and tossed them aside. She kicked the trough, sending it flying off the platform. A couple of the men dove to catch it. "Kane? Can you hear me? Wake up."

She lifted the blaster and pressed it to the rope

hoisting him up. Firing once, she tried to catch his weight, but he fell heavily against her and tumbled to the floor headfirst.

"Watch, our leader will rise," Giant insisted. "He'll show us the true power of the blood magic. This is what he wants!"

"Blood. Blood. Blood..." the chant whispered over them.

Nova pointed the blaster at the crowd in warning, but they didn't challenge her. Their eyes remained fixed on Doyen as if not wanting to miss their miracle.

"Nova," Doyen whispered.

Nova knocked her brother's knife away before rushing to pull the darts from Roderic. She kicked his trough aside and shot the cat-shifter free. She tried to keep him from landing on his head as he thumped onto the platform. She again aimed her gun at the crowd.

Nudging Roderic with her foot, she ordered, "Wake up!"

Giant pushed back his hood and stepped closer. He stared intently at Doyen as his lips moved in their sick chant.

"Blood. Blood..."

Nova pointed the gun at Giant. She wondered

why the small crowd didn't charge her in defiance now that their leader was down. Needlessly, she warned, "Stay back."

She returned to Kane.

Doyen had fallen forward, bracing his weight with one hand while holding up the other to keep the men back. That one action probably saved her from retaliation. His hand dropped to support his weight.

"Blood. Blood..."

Nova kneeled between her brother and Kane, careful to stay out of Doyen's reach. She tried to examine the cut on the prince's bloody arm but had no way to bind it.

"Nova," Doyen said, a little louder.

Nova looked at her brother's back as he remained on his hands and knees. Blood coated his clothing. "Blast it all, Doyen. Why didn't you stop? Why did you make me shoot?"

Doyen gave a wry laugh. "Have you ever known me to back down?"

"Blood. Blood..."

He collapsed forward on the floor. The chanting stopped.

"He'll heal," someone insisted. "Watch."

The room became quiet.

"Tell them to get you a handheld medic," Nova insisted into the silence. She placed the blaster on the ground next to her and flipped Doyen over onto his back to plead with him, "Please, Doyen, this isn't a game. They'll obey you."

The shot had gone through his body, and he bled from his stomach. She pressed her hands to the wound. Her brother moaned. He coughed, and blood trailed down his cheek.

"I don't know how to fix this." Nova kept her hands over the wound. She glanced at Kane and Roderic. Both of them bled, but their cuts appeared less critical. However, they still weren't moving. There was only one of her. She didn't know what to do. Tears rolled down her cheeks. She reached for Kane's arm, trying to stop his bleeding with one hand as she pressed Doyen's stomach with the other.

"Roderic, get up!" she begged, unable to reach the cat-shifter. "Kane, get up. I need you to move. Please, I don't know how to fix this."

Eyes remained focused on them from the followers.

"What are you staring at? They need a medical booth," Nova yelled at the Blood Fanatics. "Or a handheld medic. Please. Someone, get help!"

"Blood. Blood..." The followers gathered closer

to the platform, crowding against it as they waited for their leader to rise.

Kane groaned. The gag in his mouth muffled his words as he ordered, "Nova, run."

She ignored the gruff command. She couldn't leave him at the mercy of this crowd.

"I said get a medic!" Nova ordered as fiercely as she could. Doyen's men didn't obey.

She let go of Kane and grabbed Doyen's face. Blood caused her hands to slip over his skin. "Order them to get help. Please."

Hazy eyes stared up at her. She saw his rueful smile as if he was somehow winning their game. But this wasn't a game.

Kane groaned again. Roderic answered the sound, finally making a noise.

"I can't feel the pain," Doyen said, a smile spreading over his face. For a moment, he looked like the young boy he'd been when she told him the story, so full of hope. Blood spread from beneath him. "The blood magic is working. I told you to have faith in me."

She held up her bloody hands to show him. "No. It's not. Your—"

"Shifters!" a panicked voice came from the back of the building. "Run!"

The men scattered like cowards until only Giant remained to stare at his leader. They tossed aside pieces of metal leaning against the wall to reveal a crawl space as they scurried to their escape.

A hand brushed her leg. Kane lay on the floor, weakly reaching for her with bound hands.

Roderic tried to push up and swayed. He collapsed.

Nova crawled for the knife and moved to cut Kane's hands free.

"Help!" she yelled, hoping the shifters would hear her.

Doyen grabbed her ankle, gripping tight.

Nova didn't know what to do. She reached for Kane's hands, lifting them while Doyen kept hold of her. She tried to cut him free.

A massive man-dragon charged into the building with a roar. The door practically ripped from its hinges under the force of his entry. Nova jolted in fright. She dropped Kane's hands and lifted the knife in automatic defense. She had never seen a dragon this big.

Giant ran after the others to escape.

Doyen's grip lightened.

Half-shifted dragons and cats rushed in behind the first, ready to battle. A cat shifted fully and went after Giant into the crawl space. The large dragon charged the platform. His yellowed eyes locked in on Nova. She froze in terror as he leaped in front of her. With a roar, he swept his armored arm against the sharpened blade, slapping it from her without injuring himself.

Nova cried out as the action tweaked her wrist. She stared at him in fright and tried to explain why she was on the floor covered in blood and holding a knife. Her voice stuck in her throat.

"Medic," was all she could manage. Tears rolled down her cheeks.

The dragon growled, and the other seemed to understand what he was saying as they converged upon Kane and Roderic.

Doyen had stopped moving. Kane grunted.

Nova lifted her hands. "Please, help..."

The shifters hoisted Kane and Roderic into their arms and carried them toward the exit. Relief filled her to know that they'd take care of the two men.

But that left her brother. They had no reason to help Doyen.

The terrifying dragon loomed over her.

"A medical booth," Nova begged as she again pressed her hands to Doyen's wound. "Please don't let him die."

The dragon took a deep breath before giving a short growl. One of the men returned and lifted Doyen off the platform. He carried him after the others.

"Thank you." Nova tried to stand. Her legs shook. "Thank—"

The dragon grabbed her by her uninjured wrist. He pulled her hand close, and his nostrils flared as if to smell the blood on her. His large hand clasped her like a manacle. Without warning, he tugged her behind him. Her feet slipped in Doyen's blood as she stumbled toward the platform and was forced to jump down.

She tried to brace her weight with her free hand, but her wrist was sore from when he'd hit the knife from her hand.

The dragon paused as she found her footing and then marched her from the building. The streets were empty as they emerged. Dots of blood marked the dirt as they followed the others. She concentrated on keeping up with the dragon warrior's furious pace as they made their way up the cliffside path.

18

Kane wanted to fight the medical booth lasers scanning his body, but the paralysis remained in his limbs. All he could manage was to move his eyes and occasionally jerk his muscles in protest. The medical booth encased him with only a small opening along the side so that he could see out. His uncles Ualan and Zoran stood over the machine like two statues, arms crossed and brows furrowed.

As the Commander of the Draig army, Zoran made a fearsome figure on a good day. He'd seen his uncle lead the charge for their rescue. If Zoran thought Nova had a part in hurting a royal family member, there was no telling what he'd do short of killing her.

As a warrior, Zoran had seen much death. The

echo of that past lingered in his eyes, a deepness that added to his authority. He had a large build that towered over others, which combined with the fierceness of a dragon. Those who met him tended to be frightened of him. Kane knew him to be a man of strict honor. He lived by a warrior's code.

Unfortunately, a warrior's code wasn't exactly friendly and forgiving.

Kane hated feeling helpless. He couldn't fight Doyen and his men. He couldn't tell his uncle that Nova had been trying to save him. All he'd been able to do was watch life unfold.

A beep sounded, and King Ualan finally moved to check the console. "The cut isn't too deep. I don't think the amount of blood you described came from him." He pushed more buttons, and the lasers' activity increased. "Sixteen punctures with the same compound we found on the alien darts confiscated from the Var marsh farmers."

"No wonder he can't move or speak," Zoran answered. "Is there permanent damage?"

Ualan didn't immediately answer as he stared at the console.

"Can the booth reverse the drug? Will he be able to speak again? Shift? Think?" Zoran asked. "His eyes move like he can hear us."

"It's too soon to tell," Ualan answered, his tone filled with worry. "The movement might be involuntary echoes."

Kane wanted to yell that there was nothing wrong with his mind. His lips wouldn't part. What if he was locked like this forever? How would he be able to protect Nova? Tell her he loved her and would do anything to be with her? How could he even propose such a thing if he couldn't move?

"Let's refrain from telling Olek and Nadja about their son until we have answers. He is alive. The rest is in the hands of the gods. Our nephew is strong, honorable, and brave. I have to believe the gods will reward that." Zoran took a deep breath and lowered his arms. The furrow in his brow lessened by small degrees.

"I will check on Roderic," Ualan said, leaving the room.

Kane met Zoran's eyes.

"If the marsh farmers are supplying darts to the Cysgodians, they will be dealt with," Zoran stated once they were alone. His words calm and deep like he conferred with his soldiers, but uneasiness lined his eyes. "We'll find the men responsible for this. They will pay. I will imprison all the Blood Faction members if necessary. You are strong, nephew. Fight this."

"She..." Kane tried to defend Nova, but the sound was faint. "She."

Zoran smiled at the noise as if relieved he tried to speak.

"She's well. She's being fed and has a place to rest," Zoran assured him.

Kane let loose a sigh of relief. He felt the drugs slowly leaving his body as the feeling returned to his limbs.

Zoran went to the console. "We need to flush your system. It's recommending you sleep."

Before Kane could try to answer, darkness overtook him.

"Send the results to the palace," Zoran ordered. "Princess Nadja will want to look over her son's health report. Send Roderic's report to Princess Tori at the Var palace."

Kane opened his eyes in confusion, trying to remember what had happened to him.

"Yes, Commander," a man agreed, followed by the sound of taps on the console. "Doing it now."

Kane groaned as he pushed at the medical booth's lid. Relief filled him as he was able to move his body. His mind clung to the fact that

Zoran said Nova was safe, but he wanted to see her.

"He's waking up," the man at the console stated.

Kane's throat was sore, and his voice cracked, "Roderic?"

Lasers automatically moved toward his neck to repair the damage.

"He lives," Zoran answered. "He had the same drugs in his system as you, plus several deeper cuts. As soon as Falke arrives and you are able to move, we will hunt down the marsh farmers together."

"Let me out." Kane's arms shifted as he pushed harder.

"Release him," Zoran ordered. "Before he breaks the unit."

The lid lifted, and Kane slid out before the unit was completely open. He nodded at Tann at the console as the dragon-shifter finished his work.

"Where is she?" Kane demanded. "I need to see her."

Zoran took a deep breath, not moving with the same urgency. "The Cysgodian? She is unharmed. Loud, but unharmed."

Zoran tossed a change of clothes at him. He motioned at Tann to leave.

Kane realized they'd cut off his clothing, and he

stood naked. He obeyed the silent command and slipped the shirt over his head before tugging on the pants.

Zoran's stern expression did not lessen, but that wasn't unusual for his uncle. "You'll need to return for a full scan later, either here or at the palace. I will not be the one to inform your mother that you did not let the booth finish. I'll face a thousand shifters in battle before I willingly face one angry Draig mother."

Kane nodded and moved toward the door, prompting Zoran to follow him. His uncle gestured that they should turn left down the corridor. The gray walls said they were in the barracks and not the stronghold at the top of the cliff.

Realizing what his uncle had said, Kane asked, "You said Prince Falke is coming here?"

Zoran nodded. "Not by my request."

Falke was Zoran's Var counterpart. The cat-shifter commander had stood opposite Zoran on the battlefield. Even though the old shifter wars were over, and there had been peace for as long as Kane had been alive, it didn't change hundreds of years of history.

Kane detected the sound of muffled conversation, and he strained to hear the distant words.

"...demand you let us pass. Do you know who I am?" The woman's voice was familiar.

"She's Lowri," another inserted.

"I'm Lowri," Lowri repeated.

"She's a faction leader," a third woman added.

"Of the Childbearers," the second woman said, as if her status should have been obvious.

"I demand I be given the largest dwelling in accordance with my station," Lowri stated.

"No." Kane recognized his cousin Lantos' resolute voice and did not envy the man.

The women gasped at his audacity and began to say as much.

"The largest suite is being allocated as a communal space," Lantos cut off their protests. "The guards will escort you back out. Home assignments will be made at a later time after sanitation and setup are completed."

Kane stopped listening to the conversation as they turned a corner. A Var guard stood in front of a door. Seeing them, the shifter stepped aside.

Kane rushed to the door and placed his hand on the scanner to open it. He hurried inside the barren space. A chair had been placed near a wall with a small table. "Nov—"

A scream cut off his words.

He took an automatic step back in confusion. Nova's young friend Tanja wielded a mug like a weapon ready to launch. He needlessly glanced around the small space, not finding Nova. Panic tightened his stomach.

Turning toward the door, he demanded, "Where is she? Where's Nova?"

A sick feeling settled inside him, and he couldn't exactly name its cause. Yes, he worried about Nova, but it felt like more than apprehension. Something was very wrong. Pain rolled through him, centering over his heart and making it difficult to breathe.

He had to get to her.

Zoran appeared in the entryway, stepping in to crowd the room. Tanja screamed again, throwing the mug at Zoran's head. His uncle swatted it away, sending it crashing against a wall. He ignored the girl's attack.

"Is this not the girl?" Zoran asked. "She appeared to tell us where you were held captive by those blood drinkers."

"Let me go," Tanja demanded. "I didn't do anything wrong."

"You're not a prisoner," Zoran answered gruffly. "There is no need for that volume."

"You are Tanja." Kane tried to keep his voice

soft and less menacing than his uncle's natural tone. "I am—"

"I know who you are. Nova sent me here to rescue you. Where is she? I want to see her." The girl tried to look brave and failed. "How come you locked me in here? I didn't do anything. You can't make me disappear."

"You were provided a safe place to rest, food, and clothing." Zoran pointed at the hand scanner on the wall next to the open door. "The exit is there. This is not a prison cell."

Tanja looked at the scanner in confusion, clearly not understanding it had been her way out. She didn't try to move past the two men.

Zoran sighed, sounding exasperated. Tanja's expression said she thought the annoyance was because of her. Kane knew it was because his uncle hated the Federation and their neglect. If the girl didn't understand simple door-opening technology in this day and age, that said plenty about her life.

Zoran went to the wall and motioned over one of the hidden drawers. Tanja gasped as it opened to neat stacks of tunics and pants.

"There should be a size for you in there." To the guard, Zoran said, "Tell Lantos we will need to provide basic lessons on how to use the facility, starting with opening doors. We don't want the population thinking we imprisoned them."

"Uncle Zoran, please," Kane insisted. "Where is the woman who rescued me?"

Zoran glanced at Tanja. "Perhaps the other woman ran. The only woman we found was covered in blood wielding a knife over you. She's being held as a combatant for interrogation."

With Zoran, that didn't automatically mean a simple conversation with Salena.

"She was distraught at being caught in the act," Zoran continued. "That one we *did* lock in a room."

"No." Kane shook his head in denial. "Nova came to save us, not hurt us. She's not a prisoner."

"Where is she?" Tanja demanded. The girl did not take a change of clothes but instead shoved the drawer closed as if to punctuate her point by denying the gift. "Where are you keeping Nova? I demand you release her."

Zoran ignored the loud girl. To Kane, he said, "Come with me. We will sort this."

Kane followed his uncle into the corridor.

"Wait. I'm coming too." Tanja hurried after them.

"That is a pathetic weapon," Zoran said, not turning around.

When Kane glanced back at the girl, he saw that she had picked up the dented mug and carried it.

"We will get you a knife, little warrior, if you can prove you know how to use it," Zoran continued.

Tanja launched the mug at Zoran's head. The old warrior leaned to the side without bothering to look as it flew past him. To Kane's surprise, he heard Zoran chuckle softly. The mug clattered down the hall.

They returned to the corridor with the medical booth rooms and walked to the end of the hall.

The hand scanner next to the last door had a restricted panel that flashed red. Zoran leaned his ear closer to the door. Kane focused his hearing, not detecting anything inside.

"It sounds like she's calmed. Enter carefully." Zoran placed his hand over the panel, and after several seconds, the door opened. He stepped aside to let Kane pass.

Nova turned at the sound, her movements sluggish. Blood stained her clothing and smeared her pale, stricken face. Red rimmed her eyes, and a bruise had started to form on her cheek.

Agony rushed through Kane, amplifying the feelings that had already begun to build as if he could feel what she felt at that moment. The deep connection took him by surprise. He'd never felt anything like it in his life.

"What did you do?" Kane whispered in shock to his uncle as he went inside the room.

"Nova!" Tanja yelled, trying to shove past Zoran.

"Easy, little warrior." Zoran put his arm to the side to block her.

Tanja cursed.

Kane slowed as he approached Nova. He could look at nothing else. "Nova?"

She blinked several times and turned her head. "He didn't..."

Kane followed her gaze along a blood trail toward a medical booth. The unit did not run. A hand reached out from within to hang limp as a body remained clamped between the lid and the bed. He peered into the shadows and found Doyen's lifeless eyes staring out at him.

"She has refused to let us take her leader's body," Zoran explained. "We were waiting for her to calm on her own. We didn't want to use the Federation's aerosol medicines without knowing how her body would react to them."

"It's her brother," Kane answered, "not her leader."

"She didn't say," Zoran said.

"Nova is a faction leader," Tanja said. "She doesn't bow to anyone."

"I..." Nova lifted her hand as if holding a blaster. Her finger jerked as if she tried to speak with her hands what her voice could not relay. Her shoulders shook, and tears rolled down her cheeks. The smell of dried blood permeated the room.

"You saved my life." Kane lifted his arms toward her, offering his embrace but not forcing it on her.

"I killed my brother," Nova finally managed, ignoring Zoran and Tanja in the doorway. "I shot him. He didn't want to get in the booth because of that story."

"You saved Roderic's life, too. It's a debt we will never be able to repay." Kane caught her against his chest as she came into his arms. He held her close. She trembled against him, so very fragile and hurt as she cried. "You had no choice. You begged him to stop. He would have killed us if you hadn't intervened—two shifters from the royal families. Our people would not let that go unanswered. You stopped a war between the shifters and the Cysgodians."

"I should never have made up that stupid blood magic story." Nova turned her head to stare at

Doyen. "I wish I could take it back. This is all my fault."

"Nova, don't talk like that." Tanja stood behind Zoran's arm blockade staring in.

Nova swiped her eyes before turning to the girl. "I'm all right. You did good. You got help." She nodded, trying to hide her obvious despair. "You did good."

"You're not responsible for other people's broken. We're all broken in Shelter City. We're all just trying to make it through the days." Tanja pushed Zoran's arm aside and came into the room. She ignored the dead body in the booth and the blood on the floor. Her expression looked wise beyond her years, much wiser than Kane had been at her age. "My mother drinks until she can't remember her own name, let alone the fact that she has me. She didn't recognize me the last time I saw her. Vace and Aten think it's hilarious to pull their pants down whenever a drone flies overhead. My generation can barely read the star language because the adults gave up on teaching us, but we know how to operate a liquor still."

Nova stopped trembling as Tanja spoke. Zoran eyed Kane holding Nova as realization dawned in his gaze. He nodded once.

"Cressida craves attention so badly that she can't stay away from the boys and is having a baby," Tanja continued. "I hate being touched or looked at. You are convinced that you have to be the Revolutionist leader even though I don't think it's what you want. As for your brother, if it wasn't blood magic, Doyen would have latched onto something else. He had a deep, empty chasm of need that could only be filled with attention and power."

"You speak well when you are not screaming," Zoran stated.

"You are condescending when you talk," Tanja quipped.

"Nova, this is my uncle, Prince Zoran," Kane introduced.

Before Nova could answer, Tanja reached for her arm. "Look at her face. She needs a medical booth."

Kane touched Nova's cheek, not wanting to let go. "Is that what you want?"

Nova tried to look at her brother.

"Not that one," Tanja said, tugging Nova out of the room with her. She led her down the hall away from her brother's body.

Nova kept hold of Kane's arm, gripping the sleeve of his tunic as if afraid he'd not come with her.

"I thought your people did not trust the medical booths," Zoran said.

"They don't. We're working on providing proof that they're safe." Nova stopped walking, forcing Tanja also to stop. She glanced back to the restricted medical booth room and took a deep breath. "Kane, I'm sorry. I found Yevgen. I didn't know what else to do. I traded him for proof that the medical booths and food simulators are safe. He said Payton gave him access to the Federation databases and—"

"She did what?" Zoran demanded.

Nova and Tanja quickly backed away from the man.

Kane frowned at his uncle. "It's been approved."

"He hasn't been vetted," Zoran insisted, evidently not pleased with the way things were being handled at Shelter City. His uncle liked order. Shelter City was chaos.

"Is that how you found me?" Kane asked.

Nova nodded.

"Yevgen has been vetted, just not discussed with all the elders. He's saved our lives more than once." Kane went to a door, not hearing the booth running inside.

"Yevgen demanded an hour of questioning me in return for that blaster. He had footage of what looked like men with tan fur dragging you into the forest, but it wasn't too clear. Then we saw the cloaked men taking you into the building." She frowned. "I need to return the weapon to him and give him the hour."

"It's true," Tanja stated.

"I'll have Payton return the weapon to him," Kane said. "The hour can wait."

Kane placed his hand on the scanner and then motioned into the room. "Nova, please lay inside the booth. I'm going to set it to do a comprehensive scan."

"I'm staying," Tanja insisted.

"No, little warrior." Zoran went to the room next door and opened it. He gestured inside. "You're getting your own scan. The plan is to schedule every one of your people once they agree. Looks like you're first in line to prove the booths are safe."

Tanja hesitated. "Does it hurt?"

"Tingles mostly. Some injections. Nothing a little warrior like you can't handle," Zoran stated.

Tanja went into the room.

"Maybe I should sit with her." Nova started to follow.

Zoran shook his head. "I will keep an eye on her."

Nova frowned but looked too tired to insist. "Tanja, I'm right here if you need me."

"Can this make me a dragon? Will I be able to fly like you?" he heard Tanja ask.

"I do not fly," Zoran stated.

"Is that because you're broken?" the girl insisted. "Or scared?"

"My generation does not fly."

"So, can this make me a dragon that flies?"

"No."

"Cat?"

"No."

"Give me bionic parts?"

"No."

"Super vision?"

"No."

"Extra arms?"

The girl kept asking questions, and Kane wasn't sure if she genuinely wanted to know or had just found a way to exasperate his uncle. He'd never seen a young one stand up to Zoran the way she did, even when she was clearly frightened by him.

"I hope your uncle has patience," Nova said.

"He's been leading the military for hundreds of years. Trust me, after that many soldiers, he has patience. And my cousins and I tried it on more than one occasion when we were her age." Kane shut the door to the room. "He must like the girl. He's answering her questions. I'm not sure of all that happened, but I'm guessing the two of them had an interesting introduction. Tanja keeps trying to throw things at him. I wouldn't be surprised if he and his wife offer to take her in as their ward."

Before he could move to the console to start the device, Nova touched his face and made him look at her. "I didn't think I'd be able to save you. Are you injured? Do you need the booth first?"

Kane held her close. "I've been checked. Everything is—"

Nova kissed him. He instantly held her against his chest and lifted her feet off the ground to keep her close. She grabbed his hair with one hand while the other dangled over his shoulder.

She smelled of blood, sweat, and dirt, but he didn't care. She was alive and in his arms. Every part of him wanted to be next to her and never let go.

His body automatically responded to the way she rubbed against him. Her thighs parted, and her legs lifted. He gave a slight bounce as he adjusted his hands to keep holding her.

The door slid open. Nova pulled back to look.

"Get out!" Kane commanded, not looking to see who was there.

The door closed. Nova resumed kissing him.

All the things he needed to articulate wouldn't come to him. He knew he wanted to convince her that they were fated to be together, but all he could think to do was deepen the kiss. He wanted to say he was sorry she'd been in danger and he couldn't save her, but her hand was in his hair, keeping him close. He needed to say he loved her, that each beat of his heart from now until eternity was only for her. But how could a man put such feelings into words?

Nova moaned softly. Her mouth moved along his jaw in tiny perfect kisses. She felt so delicate against him, as if he could break her if he held her too tightly, but he had seen her great strength firsthand.

"I want to feel," she whispered against his ear. "Let me feel you."

How could he deny her? Why would he want to?

Kane gently set her down so he could pull his shirt over his head. He pushed his loose pants off his hips. Her tighter clothing took more time, but watching the unveiling was as erotic as feeling her. His eyes roamed the curves of her body, sure he'd never seen anything so beautiful. Then he detected a bruise on her hip and frowned.

"You need the medical booth." He went to the console to turn it on. His passion would have to wait.

"Don't." Nova slipped a hand over her shoulder. Naked flesh pressed against his back. "Not yet."

He was hers to command.

19

Nova didn't care about her bruised body and sore wrist. She held on to Kane, needing to feel the connection to him. It pulled at her, deep and painful, as if stepping away would equal ripping off her own skin. She pressed her chest against his back to feel him breathe. His heat soaked into her and calmed the trembling. His smell erased that of blood and dirt.

The fear she'd felt on that platform had shaken her to the core, knocking loose all the stupid concerns she'd carried her entire life. Who cared what her people thought of Kane? Who cared if she chose to be with a shifter? If they didn't want her to lead because of it, so be it. She didn't need to be a leader to fight for them. She could still prove that the medical booths and food simulators were safe to use.

The family legacy had condemned her brother to his delusions. It could have easily done the same to her. It had made her deny her attraction to Kane out of a sense of duty to the past.

"I need to feel anything but sadness and grief," she whispered. "Being with you is the first time I can remember that I felt safe since I was a child."

He turned to face her. His eyes flashed with golden inner fire. "I'm sorry I didn't protect you."

Nova didn't want to talk about what happened. She wanted to erase it from her mind, if only for a moment. She took a deep breath and glanced down. The strength of his erection said he was interested in more than conversation. He touched her cheek, running his fingers lightly down her throat and between her breasts to her stomach.

Nova leaned into him, lifting her mouth for a kiss. His arousal brushed her stomach, and she felt his body tremble in response. Stiff muscles forced her breasts to mold against them, pressing into her nipples.

Kane held her gently, as if afraid he'd hurt her. He ran his hands over her back and hips, careful not to press too hard against the bruises. In contrast,

Nova clung to him, holding on tight for fear the moment might slip away. She ignored her sore wrist as she tangled her fingers into his hair.

Pleasure erupted inside her, moving from his kiss like a hot rush of awareness down her body. Every inch of her tingled. She leaned into that feeling, into the mindlessness that it promised.

This time when he lifted her off the ground, she wrapped her legs around his waist. The only place to lie down was in the medical booth. He carried her over and placed her gently on the smooth, hard surface. The lid hovered above them, ready to clamp down on command. He braced a knee next to her thigh while keeping one foot planted on the floor. There wasn't enough room for them to lay comfortably together, but she didn't care.

"I'm sorry I ran from you last time," she said when his mouth left hers.

"It was more of a walk." A slow smile curled his lips. "You're back now."

Their eyes locked, and he entered her slowly. Their breaths mingled, a private song only for the two of them, a soft exhalation to drown out all the chaos and noise of their lives.

Don't go.

Don't stop.

Jump.

Nova wanted to lock them away in this perfect moment. She didn't care that the unforgiving bed didn't allow for unrestricted movement and pressed against her bruises, or the room smelled stale like someone had sealed it away from fresh air, or that the lights intermittently flickered.

She lifted her hips to meet Kane's. The first time against the tree had been a frenzy, a cumulation of repressed desires. Now the frenzy stirred from the idea that she'd almost lost him. She grabbed his waist and pulled him into her. She tried to quicken their pace, but he stayed gentle, rocking into her body with maddening slowness.

Kane's lips brushed against hers.

"Please," she begged into his mouth. "I'm not going to break."

Kane thrust a little harder and deeper. Nova gasped in approval and nodded. He did it again.

The tenderness remained as he gave her what she wanted. Pleasure rippled through her, causing her to tremble. Suddenly, she tensed, every muscle stiffening as she met her climax. Kane moaned as if he'd been holding himself back. He froze over her, hands braced on the medical booth to hold his weight, and he met with his release.

Nova's leg fell to the side, and her foot landed on the floor close to his. For a long moment, he stayed over her, limbs tangled in the small space. His eyes stared into hers as if searching deep inside her thoughts.

"I feel you," he said.

Somehow the words made sense. She imagined she could feel him too. A calm radiated from him, pulsing into her in undulating waves. She felt cared for, protected, loved.

Loved?

Maybe her imagination was getting away from her. He had said nothing about love. Nothing had changed in their worlds. The Federation still loomed. Shifters were trying to figure out what to do with their new wards. Cysgodians didn't trust the shifters. Factions were struggling for power.

"I know there are many barriers that must be dealt with." Kane eased himself out of her and moved to sit on the edge of the medical booth beside her. "However, I need you to know if you but say the word, I will wait until the end of time for us to cross them and find each other. You are the only one for me, Nova. Say you will have me, and I will do anything you ask of me. If you want me to live as a Cysgodian, I will. If you want to live with the shifters, we can. If you want to leave this planet, I will find us the next ship off-world. If you want me to wait for peace, then I will wait."

"Kane, I...?" She tried to sit up, but he put a hand on her shoulder to keep her on her back.

"You must stay in the booth. I should have waited until after your examination." He stood and went to the console.

She watched him in shock over his words. Did he just say he wanted...?

"Kane, I don't understand. You want me to...?" Hope dared to rise from the confusion.

"I wish to make you my wife," he stated.

The medical booth's lid started to lower over her. She tried to push up, but her sore body protested, and she settled back to let the machine lock her inside.

"But you're..." She tried to peer out at him through the gap left on the side of the booth. "And I'm..."

"A dragon and a Cysgodian?"

"Prince and faction leader," she corrected.

"I understand it's complicated for you."

Lasers appeared and moved over her body. Nova felt their warmth as they scanned her for injuries.

She reached her hand out of the booth and wiggled her fingers. "Kane?"

He instantly appeared and took her hand. "Don't be frightened. I'm here. It's doing the initial health scans before prioritizing what to heal."

Kane guided her hand back inside the booth and knelt on the floor next to her, where she could see him.

Nova tried to keep hold of him, but he let go.

"I don't want to confuse your results." He remained next to her. "I have gone through this process many times, and it won't hurt. You'll be asleep for part of it."

"What did my brother and his people do to you?" she asked. "Why couldn't you move or speak?"

"Paralytics." He glanced around before finding his pants. "The drugs were inside the metal darts. We were fortunate you pulled them out of us when you did. You saved us."

Nova watched him stand to pull the pants on before again sitting on the floor next to her in what appeared to be a more comfortable position. Unable to help herself, she reached for him again. She touched his shoulder with the back of her hand. "Don't leave."

Kane gently guided her hand back into the booth. The console beeped, and she felt a sting against her butt. She gasped in surprise.

"I'll be here," he whispered.

His face blurred, and her vision darkened as she was pulled into a deep sleep.

"WE'RE LUCKY THE FEDERATION ALREADY HAD Cysgodian biology installed in the units. Olek told me the Medical Alliance has put them on the near-extinction list and thus will only be available in the humanoid archives."

Nova recognized King Ualan's voice.

"The little warrior must have been in much pain," Zoran stated, the sternness of his tone unmistakable. "But she did not complain once."

Was that pride in the scary dragon's voice?

What kind of strange dream was this?

Nova struggled to open her eyes, but her lids were too heavy. Her limbs wouldn't move.

"The booth recommends we monitor her treatments. She'll need several visits," Zoran continued.

"The disease is eating her bones from the inside out. They would have become brittle enough to break at the smallest impact in another year. In the best conditions, she would have died in five. In Shelter City..."

Zoran let his words trail off.

"It is good we caught it," Kane said.

Realization dawned as Nova became more aware of her surroundings. This wasn't a dream. Little warrior was what the giant dragon called Tanja.

She tried to speak, but only a soft gasp of breath left her mouth.

"I wish to make her my ward," Zoran said.

Kane had said something about his uncle probably doing that. What did it mean?

"I have spoken to Pia, and she has agreed," the dragon continued. "We will be able to monitor her care at the palace. It is not too late to see to her education and training. The girl showed bravery in coming to the facility alone and honor in doing so to help Kane and Roderic."

"Is that what she wants?" Ualan asked.

"She's a child. I have not asked her." Zoran's matter-of-fact tone did not change. "But I believe it is what is best for her. We will be able to modify any training in accordance with her medical updates."

"For the sake of relations with the Cysgodians, we must give Tanja a choice," Kane said. "We can't be seen as stealing their young ones even if her mother is too drunk to recognize her."

"Either way, I will take it upon myself to ensure she is cared for," Zoran said.

Nova finally managed to open her eyes. Lasers moved along her neck and down her chest.

Her naked chest.

Surprised by the realization, she glanced to the side to see if Kane's uncles could see her nudity. A privacy cloth had been draped over the booth and covered the opening. Shadows fell onto the dark material, but the details were obscured.

"Regardless of what Tanja decides, we should send her medical records to my mother, and those from anyone else we can convince to get into these booths," Kane said. She instinctively knew which shadow belonged to him. "We already have Justina's medical information. When the Federation arrives, they will have to account for the documented neglect. We might be able to use that to keep them off this planet for good."

"Truth is the truth," Zoran stated.

"I agree. The truth will only serve to help all of us," Ualan said.

"What about this one?" Zoran asked. "She's been in there for twelve hours."

Nova frowned, torn between wanting to hear the answer and not wanting them to discuss her like some kind of test subject. She had no way of knowing if twelve hours was a long session in a medical booth, but Zoran's tone indicated they had cause for concern.

"The injuries she received when she saved my life were fixed first," Kane said. "The full-body workup should be almost completed."

She heard the sound of someone at the console. After a moment, the king said, "The report indicates that most of the health issues have to do with malnourishment. That is to be expected. There were a few growths of concern and an imbalance."

"They've been corrected," Kane said. "I've been monitoring her progress closely."

"I have no doubt." Zoran sounded amused, if such a thing was possible.

"She's waking up," Ualan said.

"Excuse us, please," Kane said. "I'd like to offer her privacy."

"You know, Kane, she didn't have to be naked

for the booth to work," Ualan chuckled. "I'll have a change of clothing sent for her."

Nova reached for the material providing her privacy and ran her fingers along it.

"I'm here," Kane said. "I didn't leave."

The material dropped past her and fell to the floor as he kneeled where he'd been when she'd fallen asleep. He had put on a tunic shirt.

"Twelve hours?" she managed, her throat sore. A numbness filled her body, and her feet tingled.

"You heard us?" Kane brought her hand to his lips and kissed the back of her fingers before placing her hand back inside. Her hand tingled like her feet as if her limbs started to wake. "It won't be much longer."

"Tanja?"

"She is better," Kane said. "She'll need to return to the booth for more treatments. Her bones have not developed properly. Did she ever mention being in pain?"

Nova shook her head. "No."

"She's a tough child," Kane stated. "As I suspected, Zoran has offered to adopt her. He's very fond of her."

Nova took a deep breath. The tingling moved up her feet as more feeling returned to her body.

"The matter will not be forced," he assured her.

"It'll be up to Tanja." She couldn't help but think it might be for the best.

"Zoran and his wife, Pia, are honorable in their intentions." He placed his hand on the edge of the booth as lasers moved along her body. His eyes drifted to where the light danced along her breasts.

"I know you would not have offered it if they weren't," she answered. "I trust you."

At that, his eyes lifted back to hers, and he smiled. "I love you, Nova. I want to marry you. I'll do it any way you wish. Now. Later. At the sacred dragon marriage ceremony on the next night of darkness. By Cysgodian custom. In space. On land. After things are settled. Before—"

"Stop rambling." Nova reached for him and touched his cheek. Happiness and fear flowed through her at his words. She thought of him hanging over the trough, so close to death. "I don't want to wait. I'll marry you now. Tomorrow is too uncertain."

Kane stood and went toward the door.

"Hey, where...?" Nova frowned and leaned her face closer to the booth's opening to watch him.

Putting his hand on the scanner, Kane opened it and glanced outside. "Come here."

Two half-shifted cats appeared in the doorway.

"Lady Nova and I are married. Tell my uncles," Kane stated, closing the door before the men could react.

Nova started to laugh, but when he turned, she saw he was serious. "Wait, did you...?"

"It is done, wife." Kane grinned. "All it takes is for both of us to state our intent."

"That's it?" Nova glanced down at her naked body. The lasers concentrated over her hip, and she felt a burning sensation. "I can't say that I spent much time imagining a day when I would marry or what dragon marriage ceremonies would be like, but I wouldn't have guessed it would be like this."

"You're not pleased." His smile fell. "Tradition-ally, we would spend the night in a marriage tent at a ceremony, after which you would crush my crystal, but you wished to be married now, and the cere-mony only takes place on the one night of darkness. It used to be that it was the only night we could marry. Of course, it used to be that women were only brought to this planet on that one night a year, so there weren't any other options. And I lost my bracelet with my mating crystal attached to it during the rebellion."

Nova had seen some of the dragons wearing

bracelets with crystals sewn on them. "That's what you were looking for by the watchtower? Your crystal?"

He nodded. "Yes. It was to glow when I found my mate. Had I not lost it, we would have seen our destiny much sooner."

The lasers shut off.

"Get me out of here," Nova ordered, pushing at the lid. It didn't release her.

"It should open soon," he said. "You are right. You deserve all the celebration of a traditional ceremony. I will make arrangements for us to share a tent. Many of the elders prefer we keep to the old ways. It will make them happy."

The lid finally moved, lifting so she could slide out. Her bare feet hit the floor, and she wobbled a little as she stood.

Kane steadied her. "I will do anything to make you happy."

Nova put her hands on his shoulders. Now that the warm lasers had stopped, the air felt cool against her naked body. The moment felt surreal. Married?

"Husband?" Nova tested the word. It sounded strange.

"Wife." He grinned. His eyes flashed with the dragon, yellowing before fading back to green.

"I don't need a tent."

A knock sounded on the door. Nova glanced down.

"Here." Kane pulled his tunic shirt off and handed it to her.

The material smelled of him, and she inhaled deeply as she pulled it over her head. When she was covered, he opened the door.

King Ualan came in carrying a pile of clothes. He bypassed his nephew and came to her. "Welcome to the family, Lady Nova."

"Oh," she answered, nodding weakly. "Thank you."

Family. Prince Kane. Did that make her a... princess? She'd momentarily forgotten that fact.

Family. Doyen. Her brother. Dead. The thought made her heart ache.

The past warred with her future. How had everything become so complicated?

The king handed her the clothes. Nova took them and tried to control the shaking in her hands. It was one thing to be with Kane the man, but to be with a dragon prince? The full impact of what that might mean began to overwhelm her.

"Please forgive us," Ualan said.

Nova forced her eyes up to look at him. "For?"

"A proper welcome into the family will have to wait," Ualan explained.

"What is it?" Kane joined her, placing his hand on her shoulder. She felt comfort in his nearness.

"Commander Falke has arrived. He and Zoran are leading some of the soldiers into the forest to track the marsh farmers. Thanks to your information about the tan fur, Nova, we know we are most likely looking for the lion brothers." Ualan looked at Kane and added, "It is expected that you and Roderic will both go with them."

Kane started to nod.

Nova shook her head. "No."

He couldn't leave. Not now. There was too much they needed to discuss. Besides, taking on marsh farmers sounded dangerous.

"This cannot be open to discussion. Your husband was seen being brought into the facility. Rumors are already spreading," Ualan said.

Your husband. How easily they accepted that title. No questions. No ceremony. The word sounded strange.

"Swift action must be taken before shifter senti-ment turns against the Cysgodians for Doyen's actions," Ualan continued. "Word will continue to spread. All progress we've made with our people will be lost if they believe Cysgodians attacked two princes. We have to contain the issue by finding the cat-shifters responsible for the darts."

Nova forced herself to steady her scattered thoughts and concentrate on the king's words. This interaction differed from their first meetings. "Why are you telling me this? Are you asking me to do something as a faction leader?"

Ualan glanced at Kane.

"He's telling you because you're now a Draig princess and a faction leader." Kane put his hand on the small of her back and rubbed gently.

"Doyen is—*was*..." Her voice caught a little, and she took a deep breath. "He's my brother."

She wasn't sure why she pointed it out. It was as if part of her tried to convince them not to trust her.

"We don't hold you accountable for his crimes," Ualan said. "And we are sorry for your loss. It cannot be an easy position. Of course, you must take time to grieve however you need."

"I need his body and a funeral pyre table," Nova said, keeping her tears in check. "I need to arrange for his funeral to show his followers, or they won't believe he's dead."

"I'll arrange for an escort to take you down to the city," Ualan said.

"No." Nova shook her head. "I don't need an escort, just a couple of men to help me carry him down the cliff."

"I want you to be safe," Kane stated. "Perhaps you should wait until I get back from the forest."

Nova frowned. "I don't need you to keep me safe. I'm in no danger from my people."

"I don't want you to be alone," he amended.

"I'll be with my people," she said.

Ualan cleared his throat. "Kane, you leave soon. The commanders are waiting."

Kane nodded. "I'll fly and catch up."

"Kane." Ualan's voice sounded firm. "They're waiting."

Kane lifted his hand and nodded that he understood. Ualan left them alone in the room.

"I think we should hold off on announcing the whole princess married thing until we've had a chance to talk," Nova said, dropping the stack of clothes on the medical booth. "There is much need to discuss."

"It's too late to take back," Kane said. "Dragons mate for life. You are my wife."

"When I said *now*, I didn't realize it would be that exact second."

His expression fell, and he looked as if she'd stabbed him.

She took a deep breath. "I'm not saying I regret it. You must admit it's complicated."

"I love you, Nova. It's as simple as that." Kane touched her cheek. "Please, don't cry. I meant it when I said I would do whatever you wanted."

He brushed his thumb over her cheek, and she felt the moisture smear. She hadn't realized the tears had fallen.

"There's so much." Nova forced a deep breath, suppressing the emotions. "My brother. The Blood Fanatics. Marsh farmers. Federation. Medical booths. Food simulators. Tanja's sick. The Revolutionists expect me to lead. There is a lot to process."

"Us?" Kane asked.

"No." Nova shook her head. "I'm not confused about us being us. I don't know what it looks like or what it will mean, but what I feel for you, Kane, that's one thing I'm sure about. I don't want to lose you."

He smiled, the look gentle. Maybe it was her imagination, but she felt his emotions rolling onto her as if they were her own.

"Then the rest is just tasks and battles. As long as we're together, we'll handle them all," he said.

Nova nodded, feeling his calmness take over her as she looked into his eyes. "You should go. The commanders are waiting."

"I don't want to leave you."

"We're leaders, Kane. What we want doesn't always matter. Our people need you to go face the marsh farmers, and they need me to handle..." She took a deep breath. "Handle my brother."

"You should not have to face that alone. I should be with you." He rubbed his hands up and down her arms.

She drank in his comfort. "Think of me, and I will think of you, and then we're together."

It was an imperfect solution, but they lived in an imperfect world. He nodded and looked as if he still didn't want to leave.

"Be safe. Hurry back." She wrapped her arms around him.

"You as well, lady wife. If you need anything, ask any shifter. Tell them who you are, and they will help you." Kane held her tight and kissed the top of her head. "I will return as soon as I am able."

21

KANE'S BODY GLIDED OVER THE TREETOPS OF THE
forest. His wings beat softly, keeping him coasting as
he searched for the marsh farmers. The large canopy
of leaves spread like flooring, hiding the dirt and
underbrush below. Only tiny paths cut through, and
they were all empty. His best hope would be to
detect a smell not natural to the forest, the pungent
whiff of their nef stills.

The Var marsh farmers received their name
from when they used to hide in the shadowed
marshes to make the illegal alcohol. Well, illegal
depending on who the current ruler had been. Some
of the farmers—like the lion brothers—had migrated
into the protected forest. Cooking nef and moonshine was dangerous, and even if they didn't drink

their product, they were always drunk from absorbing the fumes.

He thought of Nova. His wife.

The very idea made the fire inside him churn in response. She'd married him. He'd been so excited that he'd announced it the moment she'd said yes. Perhaps it would have been better if he waited for her to get out of the medical booth. Then again, why wait? He didn't want a second longer to go by without claiming her as his mate. They were fated to be together. He didn't need a crystal to tell him that.

Kane flew lower, eager to flush out the marsh farmers so he could return to Nova's side. He didn't want her to be alone. She put on a brave face, but he felt her sorrow and guilt as real as if they were his own—worse since he could do nothing to ease the burden from her heart. Even over the distance, he felt her inside of him. That was what it meant to have a mate. The elders and his married cousins had said that would happen.

He closed his eyes and tried to send her a feeling of love to let her know she wasn't alone.

His feet brushed the treetops, and he instantly jerked himself up to correct his flight path. Kane forced his senses to concentrate on the task at hand.

Time held frozen as he searched, scanning the

expanse of green leaves and breathing deeply. Roderic, Falke, and Zoran led a handful of soldiers on the ground. He listened for the whistle that would come if they found the farmers first.

The pungent smell of a still hit him and then disappeared. He dove forward, circling and twisting around to pick up the scent. When he caught it, he noted the location and flew to the nearest opening in the trees to land.

Kane let his body half shift as he came close to the ground. Wings retracted, and his bones cracked to force his body upright as he dropped to the dirt path. The hard armored skin of the dragon protected him as he walked like a man. He faced the direction his companions traveled from and let a low, steady growl sound in the back of his throat to signal the others.

Kane listened. When he didn't receive an answer, he tried again.

Zoran's low growl sounded faintly in response.

With luck, the still farmers would be passed out, and he'd be able to creep up on them undetected.

Kane stepped off the path into the dense underbrush of the woods. He'd track the location and then come back to meet the others. His feet moved stealthily over the forest litter.

The wind whistled through the branches, inter-rupted by the groaning crackles of the swaying wood. The canopy of leaves only let tiny spots of light through. He navigated through the forest, pausing to hide behind the bubbly texture of thick trunks to listen for the farmers. The gentle rustling of animals sounded somewhere in the distance, but the soflair did not sing. The fact that the birds were not in the area was telling. They avoided the stills.

The forest was in Var territory and had primarily been left undisturbed, and the wild beauty of mossy overgrowths, fallen tree trunks, and untamed vines created secret nooks. The trees had grown unham-pered for centuries and were as wide as a small spacecraft. It had only been in recent decades that the marsh farmers began encroaching on the area.

Kane moved from tree to tree, trying to catch the scent he'd detected from above. Every sense was on alert, focused on potential dangers.

"Stop," a voice commanded.

Kane froze at the sound.

"Pour slower," the same voice said.

Kane took a deep breath. The order had not been for him. He crept toward the sound.

"They're more trouble than they're worth," a

second voice grumbled. "This was a bad trade, two for two. Let's bury them and be done with it."

A woman whimpered, and a series of thuds followed the noise.

Kane quickened his pace, moving faster to find the source of the conversation.

"Ow," a woman gasped.

The men laughed.

"She needs a bandage," a second woman demanded. "Atria, you shouldn't be bleeding like this."

Kane detected the faint smell of blood but didn't need it to track the location. The woman's loud voice had cut through.

No one had warned him that women might be at the lion brothers' campsite. It was possible he'd found the wrong still.

"Just let Shaula and I go. We'll go back to the city," Atria pleaded.

The men laughed harder, the kind of maniacal sound the inebriated made.

"You trespassed into our land. We did not invite you. You're free to wander off and starve at any time," one of the men responded.

"If a starving creature doesn't eat you first." A

roar followed the taunt. The women yelped in response.

"Stop!" Atria cried.

Kane heard the woman's fear and didn't think. He leaped onto a fallen log and surveyed the clearing below. Two large cylinders stood over fires, with a third pulled open. Ingredient containers lay strewn around it.

A lion shifter dangled a woman before him as he held her up under her armpits. The cat was half-shifted, and the woman dressed like a Cysgodian. Black markings along her temples confirmed it. She kicked her legs to be let free, but each time her toes landed against the shifter's thighs, it made him laugh harder.

"Fergal, let her go." Atria stood cradling her bloody hand. She too had the temple markings of a Cysgodian though she wore one of the tunic shirts stored in a watchtower for the dragons.

Kane looked for the weapon that had caused her wound, only to find a smear of blood along the lid of the empty still. A large lion lay in full cat form on the ground, limbs sprawled as he slept. He assumed the cat was Valter. His size fit the description. So much for the shifter having been killed. Payton had been right. The report of his death had most likely been a ruse to interrupt their first meeting with the Cysgodian faction leaders.

Kane frowned. There had been two male voices. If Fergal had the woman, that meant Curtis had to be around somewhere. He listened to the forest for the missing cat. Awareness prickled his nerves as he heard the soft crunch of twigs.

Fergal tossed Shaula toward Atria. The woman tried to catch her friend, but they both tripped over the nef supplies on the ground and landed with a thud.

Valter roared and stirred in protest as a metal container rolled into him but was soon back asleep. The women scrambled to their hands and knees and stayed close together on the ground.

"I didn't see anyone. The dragons were probably passing through on their way to the city. Nothing to be alarmed about." Curtis appeared from the trees in the form of a man. Dirt smudged his body, and his pants hung loose on his hips. "Stop playing with the servants. The buyers expect a full load."

"They're slowing us down," Fergal answered, clearly not as concerned as his brother about possible dragons in the forest. "Watching them takes more work than doing it ourselves. They already ruined one batch by letting the fires go out." He motioned at Atria. "This one can't even lift the bags."

Atria glared back at him.

Kane listened to the woods for the others. They would be expecting him to meet them so they could converge on the campsite together. But he couldn't leave.

Fergal ignored her. "I'm bored with them. If you won't let us claim them, then we have no use to keep—"

Curtis darted forward, his body half shifting to give him power before he backhanded Fergal. His brother spun before sprawling on the ground. Curtis pointed at him. "If you even think of putting your prick into one of these diseased aliens, I will cut off the tainted appendage in your sleep before it rots off."

The man walked over to the sleeping lion and kicked him. "Valter, get up. We need two holes."

The women whimpered and huddled closer together.

Fergal drew a knife and rolled up from the ground. A sinister expression crossed his features as he took Curtis' words as permission. He smiled and pointed the blade at the two women.

Kane glanced behind him. No one was coming.

"Get up," Fergal ordered.

The women cried out and refused, crawling away from him.

Things escalated quickly. Fergal laughed and drew his arm back to throw the knife.

Kane didn't hesitate. He leaped down from the high log with a roar. The noise was enough to startle Fergal. The cat-shifter's throw went off target and landed in the dirt next to Atria. The woman screamed and hurried away from the blade.

Instantly, Curtis and Fergal charged him. Valter made strange grumbling noises as if fighting to come awake.

Kane growled as he lurched forward to meet the attack. Claws glanced over his armored skin seconds before their shoulders made an impact against his. He drew his arms between the brothers' bodies and shoved them to the side as hard as he could. They flew in opposite directions.

"Run," Kane growled at the women. The sound of his gruff voice terrified them, and they gasped. He pointed toward the trees.

Valter staggered drunkenly to his paws and shook his head as if to clear his mind.

The women glanced wide-eyed at each other before scrambling toward the trees. Kane heard them struggling to climb through the thick underbrush.

Curtis and Fergal rolled on the ground and came up on all four paws. Valter joined them. The three cats surrounded Kane. It would be easy to shift into a full dragon and spout fire to end the fight before it started, but he would not risk burning down the old forest.

Curtis and Fergal leaped in unison, forcing Kane to defend himself. He punched Fergal in the jaw. The lion's head snapped back. Curtis latched his teeth on Kane's arm. The force of the bite cut past his hardened skin.

Kane stumbled and pounded his fist into Curtis' side, trying to dislodge him. Valter took advantage of his compromised state and pounced. They fell into a heap of slashing claws and talons. The lions wrestled Kane to his back. They clamped down on his arms, pulling them roughly to each side as if to try and tear him apart. Fergal charged his center.

Kane roared in anger. He kicked both feet off the ground and planted them squarely on Fergal's face. The lion flipped backward with a pained yelp. A loud clang sounded as he made contact with a still. Kane's feet landed, and he instantly kicked again, this time spreading his legs wide while he tried to draw his arms down to his sides. Valter lost his hold.

The smell of liquor became potent, and the cooking fires from beneath one of the stills sizzled. The hot blaze roared to life, crackling as it found fuel in the dried leaves on the forest floor.

Kane rolled, ignoring the sharp pain of Curtis' bite and the blood trailing from his wounds. He wrapped his arm around Curtis' neck and began choking him. When the shifter's jaw jerked, Kane ripped his arm out of the lion's mouth.

Orange firelight glowed over them, and there was nothing he could do to stop it. The flames roared higher.

Valter renewed his attack. Kane swung Curtis around by his neck and into Valter's path. When Valter slammed into his brother, Kane released his hold and sprang to his feet.

"Kane!" Zoran yelled, the gruff dragon's tone cutting through the sound of the blaze. He stood in his dragon-man form on the fallen log perch where Kane had surveyed the campsite. He pointed toward the fire.

Kane held his bleeding arm and pushed to his feet. Fergal wasn't moving, and the fire came danger-ously close to consuming him. Kane lurched for the shifter's leg and dragged him away from the flames. He slapped his hands against singed fur to stop it from burning more.

Zoran roared and jumped to the forest floor to face Curtis and Valter. Roderic appeared in full cougar on the log before leaping down. As Zoran wrestled Valter to the ground, Roderic ran at Curtis. The cats reared and met each other in slashing battle.

Prince Falke jumped over the log and landed near Roderic. The white tiger instantly forced his nephew aside as he took over the fight. The Var commander had Curtis on the ground with his fangs over the shifter's throat. Falke growled in warning. Curtis didn't move.

Zoran punched Valter several times, only stopping when the lion stopped moving.

Three more dragon-shifters joined them. The guards were of the older generation and could not shift into full dragons. Since the fire did not affect dragon skin, the guards instantly began running to tamp out the blaze. Their clothing caught fire, but they ignored it.

Kane let his inner animal take over. When the dragon had taken shape, he charged toward the fire and rolled over it, smothering most of the flames. His tail sent the last full still flying as he rolled over its cooking fire. The leaves dangling over the clearing had withered some, but the fire had not spread up into the branches.

He took up too much space in the enclosure as a full dragon. Kane felt his bones cracking as he returned to a half shift. Soot and dirt clung to his naked body, mixing with the blood coating his arms.

Prince Falke stood from the ground as a man and ordered the dragon guards, "Tie them and take them back to the facility."

Though Valter and Curtis' eyes were open, the lion brothers lay unmoving.

Falke and Zoran were two of the most imposing shifter figures, matched not only in skills but in great size. It wasn't too hard to imagine why they had been named commanders during the old war. The guards glanced at Zoran for direction. The dragon commander nodded that they should obey the cat-shifter.

"Roderic," Falke continued. "Find those Cysgodian women so we can escort them back to Shelter City."

Roderic shifted and stood. "Kane's injured."

"Go," Falke ordered.

Roderic obeyed, jogging naked into the forest.

Zoran took off his tunic shirt and used his talon to cut it in two. He tossed half of it to Falke. He shifted into human form as he approached Kane.

"You fought well," Zoran said with approval. He wrapped his shirt around the bite wound on his arm.

Falke nodded once in agreement and bound the other arm. They pulled the bandages tight.

Kane grunted. Now that the fight was over, the pain made itself known.

"Can you fly?" Zoran asked.

Kane nodded.

Zoran sighed. "Then let's get you back to the path, and you can fly ahead of us. Your mother won't be pleased you need a medic so soon after the last time. I'm inclined not to mention this incident to her, or she might never let you leave the palace."

22

Nova didn't wonder at the tightness in her chest. She expected the feelings of grief and loss and guilt to fill her as she pushed the funeral pyre with her brother's body through the city streets. The pyre table hovered from the ground, making the trip smooth. It was the one piece of equipment the Federation let them use that actually worked. A sheet covered his corpse, but blood had seeped into the white material, leaving a stain that stared back at her like an accusation.

What she didn't expect was the horrible pain in her arms. The table wasn't heavy, and she didn't strain as she walked behind it, but her arms ached. Her skin felt like tiny invisible knives cut into her. Fear followed the sensation, and she thought of

Kane. The urge to run into the forest after him was great.

He is with the others. He'll be safe.

The thought gave little comfort.

Nova glanced back for her shifter escorts. They had stayed behind, watching her from the cliffside path. The fact surprised her. They'd been insistent on following her up until the moment she'd ordered otherwise.

Being a princess clearly came with perks.

Nova took a deep breath. She'd been so judgmental of Justina for her position as a Var princess. Now she realized some of it had been jealousy. Justina had found happiness, a rarity in Shelter City.

Nova looked at the group assembling to watch. Their murmuring voices rolled over the marketplace as word spread of the funeral walk. She wondered what they would think if they knew she was a princess now.

She had yet to come to terms with the idea.

Nova glanced into the distance, trying to see where Tanja had disappeared into the city. The girl said nothing about her pain being gone and had shrugged off the question when asked. Zoran had told the girl to stay in her room at the stronghold facility when he'd left. It probably hadn't occurred to the commander dragon that he wouldn't be obeyed. When Nova had gone to retrieve Tanja, no one had stopped them from leaving.

"Who is it?" someone asked. "Who died?"

People stepped into her path in their curiosity, forcing her to stop. They drew closer.

Nova took the sheet, gently lifted it over Doyen's head, and folded it onto his chest. She couldn't look at his face and watched the others' reactions instead. A gasp of surprise erupted, followed by the word being spread. Pieces of the conversations filtered to her from the crowd.

"Faction leader Doyen."

"It's the Blood Fanatic."

"Doyen."

"Doyen."

"...dead..."

Nova took a shaky breath and glanced at her brother's pale face. Tears formed in her eyes.

"What happened?" someone demanded. "It can't be him. He drank the blood magic!"

The crowd gathered closer. This was not how she wanted to do this.

"Clear a path." Jare appeared, pushing his way through the crush of people. He stopped near

Doyen's feet. He studied the fallen faction leader's face for a moment before nodding at Nova. Softly, he muttered, "Fools and dreams."

Nova wasn't exactly sure what he meant by that, but she nodded once.

Jare turned to the others and ordered, "Show respect. Let Nova pass for her brother's death walk. To lose one of us is to lose any of us."

Eyes turned to her as if they would protest their unanswered questions, but one by one, they slowly backed away to let her continue. Nova pushed the funeral table forward as Jare walked before her, taking the lead. Though he had not been invited to head the procession, she was grateful that he commanded enough respect to navigate through the crowd. As an elder, he'd walked for many funerals. The onlookers quieted and fell into step behind her.

The constant clanging of metal rings against a pole created a lonely song that seemed to mark each step. The occasional murmur broke through the silence but quickly quieted.

Jare led them past the marketplace toward the storage buildings. Nova glanced down the street toward Yevgen's hideout and wondered if he was watching them. She looked toward the sky, not spotting any drones.

Jare stopped walking when they reached their destination, a wide section of the open street. Nova stared at her brother's face, not really seeing him. She saw her father dying on the other side of the glass, blood streaming down his face. She remembered the streets lined with bodies, so many bodies. She thought of her starving mother. And now, her brother went to join them in whatever was beyond the physical confines of this life.

"Nova?" Jare joined her.

She blinked, realizing they expected her to speak.

"I am Nova. I will speak for the dead." Her voice wavered, and she cleared her throat. Louder, she added, "I will speak for my brother."

What did she say? What could she say? The truth?

I'm sorry I killed him.

Everyone knows he was a bully and a slargnot. I spent most of my adult life hating him and embarrassed by him.

Blood magic isn't real.

Doyen died a fool.

None of those words would form, and instead, she said, "I wish you could have known my brother when he was young, on Cysgod, before Shelter City tarnished him. I know we don't like to talk about the old days, especially at times like this, because that loss is still too great to measure. But maybe we should talk about that loss."

Eyes turned away from her, and others openly frowned at the suggestion. Mensa and Celestial pushed their way to the front.

"We should remember who we were before and whom I believe we might be again. Doyen forgot. He told stories about blood magic and convinced people that he stepped on the path to immortality." She gestured at him. "He was not wrong to hope for better, but he was wrong in thinking this was the path to find it. So strong were his convictions that he refused a medical booth. This is the result. I accepted the medical booth, and I stand here before you."

"This is not the time for politics," Jare said, his voice low.

"It is the time," Nova disputed. "I speak for my brother."

"Let her speak." Mensa came closer to lend her support. Celestial followed her, less confident. Liberation appeared next to them.

Jare nodded and backed away, bowing his head.

"I loved my brother," Nova continued. "And I

hated who he became. I hate what this city turned him into. I hated that part that needed to tell stories of blood magic, even as I understand the need for fairy tales. But the time for fantasy is over. This is the real world, and we have the opportunity to build a real future."

"Let me see him!" Giant pushed his way through the onlookers. An angry cut showed on his bare arm. He did not wear his hooded cloak. She recognized other Blood Fanatics also out of their usual costume and wondered if their failed attempt to murder two princes had made blending into the Cysgodian population necessary.

Giant glared at Nova before he took in Doyen's face. He whipped the sheet off the body and placed his hand over the bloody clothing. "I will speak for my leader."

"We already have a speaker for the dead," Jare interrupted. Blood Fanatics overtook the crowd, spreading throughout the people to intimidate.

Giant ignored the older man. "Faction Leader Doyen was a great man."

The Blood Fanatics cheered, forcing some of those around them to lift their arms as well.

"He saw a path for us, one where we controlled our own destinies," Giant continued. "With freedom. Where we took rule of this planet away from the animals! They killed him—"

"I speak for my brother," Nova interrupted. "I shot—"

"I speak for my leader," Giant argued. "And—"

"Estimates show that they will all be dead in twelve years, and we'll no longer have a Cysgodian concern."

Loud disembodied words boomed over them. Nova looked up, trying to see where the sound came from. The sky was clear.

"That's the general," a woman said, panicked. "That's his voice."

"Once the virus clears, and the planet is ruled safe to inhabit, which our researchers indicate should be in about a hundred years, there will be no descendants left to lay claim to Cysgod. I believe the Federation is morally obligated to take over planetary rights."

Lights flickered, and General Sten's face showed large on the side of the building. Nova again glanced around, looking for the source of the movie. Tanja appeared from the direction of Yevgen's home. The girl made her way quickly around the crowd toward Nova.

"We tried to give them medical screenings, but

they refuse to use the booths," the general's projection continued. "Our scientists are starting to notice a strange side effect of the virus in the form of aggression within the population."

The general disappeared, and scientific charts emerged in his place. Nova frowned, unable to read what the formulas meant.

The show continued.

"Sell the food," a soldier stated as he stood in an alleyway. His nametag read, "Sever."

The image froze and skipped, the quality not as good as the general's face had been.

Sever held out his hand to show a vial of black liquid. "Put one drop of this in it before you do. When the vial is empty, come back for a refill. But don't try to pour it out. We'll be able to tell if it's not distributed."

"What is it?" the merchant Yellow Shirt inquired as he appeared on the wall.

"Vitamins and a few other things. Does it matter?" Sever asked.

Yellow Shirt shook his head in denial.

Sever appeared inside the stronghold facility, the image sharper than the alleyway. "One drop into the food of your target and then get out of the area. Any more than that, and it'll be too obvious."

Justina hesitated as Sever gestured for her to move. They stood inside a white prison cell.

"You should know the medical scan found several abnormal growths," Sever threatened. "The growths won't kill you right away, but..."

The appearance of Sever's large projected smile caused Nova's skin to crawl as the image froze.

"What does it mean?" one of the watchers asked, voicing the confusion showing on several faces.

"Yevgen decided he wanted to speak for the dead," Tanja whispered, coming to stand next to Nova. She held out her hand to show the old Cysgod newspaper chip. "He said to tell you that the information trade is complete."

Tanja slipped the chip into her pocket for safekeeping. Nova put her hand around the girl's shoulders and hugged her against her side. They watched the wall.

"Can you fix them?" Justina's image asked as the show began to play once more.

"I can." Sever nodded. "But I find people work harder when there is an incentive to do so. You distribute that whole vial and come back for a refill. We'll take care of one of the masses for you. And, in case you lose your nerve or happen to get caught, remember, I'm your access to a medical booth, and it will be in your interest to stay quiet."

"Who?" Justina lifted the vial, and the projection zoomed in on the dark liquid.

"Anyone with a short temper and preferably great strength," Sever answered. "Around crowds are best. The more chaos, the better."

The show again froze. Nova wondered if Yevgen was having trouble with the signal.

"The Federation poisoned us?" Jare whispered, more to himself. "They're responsible for the food sickness?"

Murmurs rose from the crowd as they tried to reason what they had heard.

"Remember, we're always watching," Sever's playback warned.

"Quiet, I can't hear," a man from the back of the crowd shouted.

Justina's image reappeared as she stood outside near the trees, holding up the vial for Prince Roderic. "I need you to tell me what this is and what it will do."

Roderic reached for the poison and balanced it between two fingers. "Where did you get this?"

"From a soldier in the facility," Justina said. "He

thought I was someone I wasn't, and I didn't correct him."

Roderic tried to pull the cap off the vial.

"Don't." Justina put her hand over his to stop him. "It might be poisonous."

Next, the projection showed Justina hanging between two posts in the middle of Shelter City. Her mouth had been gagged, and her hands cuffed and tied over her head so that her feet dangled over the ground. Word of the Federation's punishment had spread through the city, and Nova would bet most of the people here had seen this event firsthand.

"Do you think they care about you?" General Sten's voice whispered over the image as a child ran and grabbed hold of Justina's legs to use her as a swing. Justina strained in agony at the horrible play. *"Do you think any of them will thank you for what you did when I cut their rations? I'll make sure they know who's to blame. Every one of them will come by to see your pretty face. And then, when I let you down and lock you in your home, well, your friends and their humanitarian medical regulations won't matter if you're murdered by your own. Do you think anyone will help the shifters after they hear about your fate?"*

The scenes came in a montage of information.

"The plan is to lay claim to the planet of Cysgod once it is inhabitable." Sever's face appeared as he sat at a table. Nova recognized Princess Salena, the truth receiver, sitting across from him. "If there are no living descendants at that time, as the last remaining governance of the Cysgodian people, the Federation Military will be able to keep the planet on their roster permanently. So we cut food rations, gave out the aggressive agent, and lied to them about the medical booths. No one will question our records if we document a slow downfall over time."

"Justina, we recognize you as the official spokesperson and first Qurilixian leader for your people. They would not be free without your bravery," King Kirill said as he stood on the cliff overlooking the city. "And your people will need a clear leader now more than ever as we move forward."

The images stopped, and the projection faded.

Nova glanced over the crowd. Silence had fallen over them, and they stared at the wall with rapt attention as if expecting there to be more.

"Yevgen kept his word," Tanja whispered.

Nova nodded. The cyborg definitely saw everything. The knowledge that they were being spied on was disturbing, but she was grateful for the evidence he presented.

A prickling of awareness started on the back of her neck, and she turned. She felt Kane before she saw him. Seconds later, the sound of running footsteps announced Kane's approach. He wore a simple tunic and had bare feet.

Kane slowed his approach as he came into view of the crowd. He looked at her questioningly. Nova smiled, relieved to see him, and reached out her hand briefly before turning back to the onlookers. Yevgen's playback had not resumed, and people were beginning to turn their attention back to the funeral pyre.

"I am Faction Leader Nova of the Revolutionists, and I speak for my brother," Nova stated, daring Giant to interrupt again. "He wanted the Cysgodians to be powerful, but he was wrong about the shifters. They are not our enemy."

Kane joined her by the funeral pyre. He looked as if he wanted to hold her but held back.

"You heard it from the Federation soldier. We don't need to fear the food simulators or the medical booths. The shifters want us to have our own power." Nova glanced at the empty wall. "I admit I was wrong about Justina, as were many of you. She risked her life to help us. Perhaps next time we should hear her out."

"But...she married a shifter," Lowri charged forward as if angry she'd missed most of the show.

Nova reached for Kane and took his hand. She pulled him close to her side. "So did I."

An uproar spread as people began to voice their opinions.

Suddenly, a loud rumble came from the table as Jare activated the pyre. Flames engulfed Doyen's body as the fire blazed. Nova stepped back from the heat.

"That's enough speaking for today. You'd better leave while you still can. Once that crowd starts to demand more answers, they'll not let you go," Jare said. "I'll stand attendance over the fire."

"He's right," Kane agreed. "I heard what was being said by that projection as I approached. You should let the information settle. We will address this when there is less chaos."

Nova nodded.

"Tanja?" Kane held out his hand and gestured that she should go with them.

Questions from the crowd cut off the girl's response.

"Wait, she said she was in the medical booth!"

"Does it hurt?"

"Nova, wait!"

"Hey, stop her!"

"What are these masses?"

"Where are these food simulators?"

Nova turned and only saw figures coming at her. The blur of movement made it hard to see who spoke.

"I promise I won't drop you." Kane grabbed hold of Tanja's and Nova's wrists and leaped into the air. His body expanded, and wings ripped from his back, tearing the clothes off his body. The hands sprouted talons, and he jerked them up off the ground. Their feet dangled, and he lifted them out of the crowd's way. His torn clothes landed on top of them.

Nova watched some of them jump and try to seize hold of her feet. She kicked and screamed in protest as Giant almost succeeded in grabbing her ankle.

Kane flapped his wings, lifting them higher. Tanja had taken hold of the dragon's wrist with her free hand as he gripped her in his taloned fist. Her eyes opened wide.

Nova did the same, gripping his wrist to help steady her weight. He lifted them over the buildings.

Even though she'd never flown, she somehow felt safe with Kane.

"It'll be all right," Nova yelled to Tanja. The cold air whipped against them.

"I love this," Tanja hollered back, though her face told a slightly different story.

Kane flew them over the valley and up to the top of the cliff by the stronghold. He lowered them to the ground gently before letting go. Nova dropped to her feet. Her legs wobbled a little, but she kept her footing. Tanja gripped Kane's arm even after he tried to drop her. Nova touched Tanja's legs as Kane lowered her closer to the ground.

"Let go," Nova said.

Tanja dropped to the ground. Nova caught her before she collapsed.

"I love flying," Tanja said.

"Sure." Nova gently rubbed the girl's back. "That's why you look like you might—"

Tanja convulsed as if she would throw up but managed to stop it. After a few deep breaths, she said, "Don't tell Zoran."

Nova nodded. "I'll tell him you were brave."

"I hope I didn't frighten you," Kane approached. He'd found another pair of pants and had pulled them on.

"My stomach did a few flops, but Tanja loves flying," Nova said with a small smile toward the girl.

"Really? I'll take you up higher next time," Kane said.

Tanja looked stricken. "That'd be...great."

Nova turned toward the city and walked to the edge of the cliff. Black smoke rose from the funeral pyre. Tanja appeared next to her and slipped her hand into hers. Kane joined them, putting his arm around her shoulders.

"I should be down there," Nova said.

"It wouldn't change the fact you're sad that he died," Tanja answered, sounding so wise for one so young. "The others would have trapped you for hours demanding answers and explanations until you had no thoughts left."

"Thank you for going to Yevgen." Nova squeezed the girl's hand as she wrapped her arm around her husband's waist. She watched the smoke, unable to help the thoughts of the past as they mingled with the present. "And thank you both for being with me now. I don't know what I'd do without you."

Kane kissed her temple. "I told you. I will always fly to you, Nova. I love you."

Nova felt his love filling her. "I love you, too."

"Yevgen said he'd keep replaying the evidence until he's sure everyone has seen it," Tanja said, ignoring their love talk. The girl looked up at the sky. "Won't you, Yevgen?"

Nova glanced up, not seeing anything.

Lights flashed softly within the city as if the cyborg answered by replaying the message near the marketplace. Seconds later, matching lights shone in three other places.

"Stop watching us, Yevgen. It's disturbing," Tanja muttered.

Nova again looked at the smoke.

"It's not your fault," Kane said as if reading her feelings. "You did the difficult thing to save many lives. Not just mine and Roderic, but Cysgodians and shifters. By saving two princes, you stopped a war between our people. You're a true leader. Remember that."

"And your deal with Yevgen brought us the truth," Tanja added. "When they feel what the medical booths can do, they'll thank you for that."

Nova studied the girl's face. "Zoran has asked to be your guardian if you wish. He'll make sure you have access to the booth to help your bones."

"I thought you were my guardian." Tanja frowned. "You always look out for me."

Nova glanced at Kane. He nodded.

"If you like, we would be honored to be your guardians," Kane said.

Tanja nodded. "I think that'd be good."

Nova sat on the ground and stared over the city. The others joined her.

Nova reached for Kane's hand as Tanja leaned her head against her shoulder. They sat in silence as they watched the fire burn.

23

"DID YOU EVER THINK WE'D SEE THIS MOMENT?"
Justina asked.

Nova stared at the long line below. They stood
on the cliff overlooking the city. Cysgodians waited
outside the barracks to be assigned housing. Behind
them, another line had formed by the stronghold
facility with people wanting medical scans. Six cat-
shifters carried giant trays with food. The amount
was more rations than many of them had seen at one
time.

Nova and Justina waited apart from the others
while their husbands questioned the lion brothers
inside one of the prison wards. Apparently, the cat-
shifters had needed time to sober up before they
could form coherent answers. Salena had gone in

with them. Nova had hidden from the truth-seeker princess. Not her finest moment, but she didn't want to be on the accidental end of another interrogation.

"I owe you an apology," Nova said.

"Oh?" Justina didn't seem too concerned.

"I judged you harshly for being with a shifter," Nova admitted. "And I dismissed you during the meeting with the faction leaders."

Justina sighed. "And now you're feeling guilty because you are a hypocrite because you too have married a shifter."

"Yes." Nova nodded.

Justina laughed. "Think nothing of it. Far crueler people have judged me for worse things. As I am sure you have."

As the morning turned to afternoon, the energy faded from fear to excitement. Scared faces now laughed as the Cysgodians tentatively joked with the shifter guards. A group of young children held up their hands like claws as they snuck up behind one of the cats. They roared loudly and quickly ran away, laughing when the guard roared back.

Nova watched as Tanja crossed over to the children and whispered to them. She pointed toward where Prince Zoran had come from inside the stronghold. The children ran toward him.

"We want to fly!"

"Take us up! Take us up!"

One of the boys jumped up and grabbed hold of an arm. The giant prince lifted his arm as if the boy weighed nothing so that the child dangled before him. His tone serious, he stated. "I do not fly."

"Did you get in trouble with your mother?" a little girl asked. "I'm not allowed to jump off buildings anymore."

"Fly!" The boy on Zoran's arm kicked his legs and swung back and forth, still holding on.

Zoran tossed the boy up and caught him under his arms. He strode toward where Nova and Justina stood. "We'll see if you can fly, little one."

The boy cried out. Zoran lifted him and began throwing him over the side of the cliff. Onlookers gasped, but he simply swung the child around and set him safely on his feet. The boy laughed as he ran to join his friends.

"My ladies." Zoran nodded in greeting at Justina and Nova.

"Prince Zoran," Justina answered. "Good to see you again."

"Do you remember what it was like to be that age?" Nova asked as they watched Zoran go back into the stronghold. "I don't know that I was ever completely fearless like that."

"It is how childhood should be," Justina answered. "We can't let the Federation come back and take it from them. I have to think there is a reason you are with a dragon, and I am with a cat. We're meant to make life better."

"Kane told me there is still no word about when the Federation will arrive, but it works in our favor if they take their time coming." Nova remembered what it had felt like to wake up next to him. She'd not wanted to leave his arms. "In the meantime, we can compile the medical data necessary to prove General Sten's neglect and abuse."

"Roderic's mother has samples of the black vial poison they used," Justina said. "There is no way they can fight the truth."

Suddenly, Justina's face lit up with a smile, and she looked expectantly at the entrance.

Nova felt Kane before she saw him. Something had happened when they married. With each passing hour, she felt more and more as if she carried him inside her.

Kane and Roderic approached.

"That didn't last long," Justina said.

"One question from Princess Salena, and they

were confessing it all," Roderic answered. "Curtis and Fergal thought the Blood Fanatics had eaten their brother. When we didn't automatically declare war on the Cysgodians on their word, they decided sacrificing two princes would be suitable payback."

Nova grimaced. "Did Doyen...?"

"No." Kane shook his head. He cupped her face and kissed her on the forehead.

"Drunk Valter got lost in the forest," Roderic explained. "But to them, the fact we didn't act was an insult."

"We did learn something about your brother." Kane appeared apologetic as he dropped his hands from her face. "He did trade with the lions. He sold them two women, Shaula and Atria, in exchange for liquor. Doyen chased the women into the forest so that they could be taken."

"The women are unharmed and in the medical booths as we speak," Roderic added.

Kane held her gaze. "He also tried to buy a shifter off of them, which is why they got it into their heads that he'd eaten Valter."

"Just tell me it's over," Nova stated. She didn't want to hear any more dark tales of her brother and his exploits.

"They'll be punished for taking the women and

for kidnapping us," Roderic said. "My uncle will escort them back to the Var palace."

"The threat is over," Kane assured her.

Nova took a deep breath and closed her eyes. "Good."

"Ah!" a girl screamed. "You're on fire, Ciro!"

More screams came from the direction of the children. Nova craned her neck as she walked toward them to see what was wrong. Ciro threw something hard. The object arched over the line of people and landed on the ground near Nova. She frowned upon seeing a tiny glowing light.

Kane's boots appeared next to it, and she glanced up.

"Hey, you found my mating crystal." He grinned.

"It's glowing." She began to reach for it. He grabbed her hand.

"You're supposed to stomp on it," he instructed.

"But it's pretty." She again began to reach for it.

"Many blessings, Prince Kane!" a dragon-shifter shouted, causing several of the other shifters to do the same.

"Many blessings!"

"Many blessings!"

The Cysgodians stopped talking and stared at them.

Kane nodded toward the ground. Nova bit her lip and stomped on the stone. She felt it crack beneath her foot. When she looked, the crystal was in several pieces and no longer glowed. A tingling sensation came over her, running up her leg to emanate along her chest and head.

Cheers erupted.

Nova took a deep breath in wonder. "That is incredible. I feel you. Completely. It's like I know everything is going to work out. You're part of me. I feel your love."

Kane grinned. "As it should be, my love. As it should be."

He pulled her close and kissed her.

The End

MEET KANE'S PARENTS

Keep Reading!
Find out about Kane's Parents

Dragon Lords: Perfect Prince

Once mated, these shifters will do anything to protect the women they love! The original Dragon Lords series' Anniversary Edition by NYT Bestselling Author, Michelle M. Pillow.

A Perfect Escape...

Nadja Aleksander has everything she could ever want in life, except her freedom. Skipping out on her engagement to a man her controlling father has chosen for her, Nadja books passage on the first ship she can find. Bound for a planet of primitive humanoid males, she plans on finding a simple, hardworking man who will allow her to live out her days in total obscurity. Unfortunately, simple isn't what fate has in mind.

A Perfect Mistake...

Dragon shifter Prince Olek is pleased with his refined and blushing bride. When she chooses him to be her life mate, appearing happy in her decision, his heart soars--until the next morning when his new princess wants nothing to do with him. The dragon prince doesn't know what he's done to upset his alluring woman, but he is determined to reignite the hot sparks that burned the night they met.

THE SERIES CONTINUES...

QURILIXEN LORDS BOOK 5

Her Lawless Prince

This fearless cat-shifter never imagined she'd become the prey.

From NY Times & USA TODAY Bestselling Author, Michelle M. Pillow, a fantasy science fiction romance!

Cat-shifter Payton refuses to be tamed by any man.

Being the adult daughter of the fiercest shifter commander on the planet does NOT have its perks. Add to that the fact that she's also a princess, and Payton has spent most of her life besting the overprotective palace guards to enjoy moments of wild freedom.

She never imagined she'd need those skills to escape with her life.

When a mysterious stranger arrives spouting conspiracies about her people's future, she's sure he needs a one-way trip to medical supervision. But the infuriatingly seductive outlaw knows things about her he shouldn't--intimate things, embarrassing things. And when one of his warnings turns real and takes them captive, Payton is made a believer. She only hopes it's not too late to save her people from extinction.

WELCOME TO QURILIXEN

QURILIXEN WORLD - FIRST IN SERIES BOOKS

**Keep Reading!
Check out these first-in-series books in the different Qurilixen World series installments!**

The Qurilixen World is an extensive collection of science fiction and paranormal romance novels by award-winning NYT Bestselling author, *Michelle M. Pillow*®. Note: Each book in each series is a stand alone story.

Dragon Lords Series: Barbarian Prince

*Dragon Shapeshifter Romance - The original Dragon
Lords series' Anniversary Edition*

Going undercover at a mass wedding as a bartered
bride, Morrigan Blake has every intention of getting
off the barbaric alien planet just as soon as the ceremony over. But the next morning, Morrigan
discovers her ride left without her and an alien
dragon shifter is claiming she's his wife. It's not
exactly the story this reporter had in mind. And to
make matters worse, the all-to-seductive dragon-
shifter alpha male refuses to take no for an answer.

Lords of the Var® **Series: The Savage King**
Cat-Shifter Romance

Cat-shifting King Kirill knows he must do his royal
duty by his people. When his father unexpectedly
dies, it's his destiny to take the throne and all of the
responsibility that entails. What he hadn't prepared
for is the troublesome prisoner that's now his to deal
with.

Undercover Agent Ulyssa is no man's captive.
Trapped in a primitive alien forest awaiting pickup,

she's going to make the best out of a bad situation... which doesn't include falling for the seductions of an alpha male king.

Dynasty Lords Series: Seduction of the Phoenix
Science Fiction Romance

A prince raised in honor and tradition, a woman raised with nothing at all. She wants to steal their most sacred treasure. He'll do anything to protect it, even if it means marrying a thief.

Space Lords Series: His Frost Maiden
Science Fiction Space Pirate Romance

Lady Josselyn of the House of Craven has been betrayed. With her home world on a Florencian moon under attack and her family dead, she finds herself at the mercy of the one who deceived them. There is only one thing left to do—die with honor. But before she can join her family in the afterlife, she must first avenge all that she held dear. Falling in love with a pirate was never in the plan. Evan and his thieving crewmates might have delayed her fate, but they can't stop destiny.

Captured by a Dragon-Shifter Series:
Determined Prince
Dragon Shapeshifter Romance

Dragon-shifter Prince Kyran has studied the Earth people and is ready to assimilate. Female shifters are all but going extinct on his planet of Qurilixen, and his people are desperate for mates—so much so they're taking matters into their own hands. What better place to find a mate than Earth? After all, dragon-shifters had come from there centuries ago. Surely a human female would be honored to be selected by one as fine and fierce as himself.

Galaxy Alien Mail Order Brides: Spark

Alien Romance

Earth women better watch out. Things are about to heat up.

Mining ash on a remote planet where temperatures reach hellish degrees doesn't leave Kal (aka Spark) much room for dating. Lucky for this hardworking man, a new corporation Galaxy Alien Mail Order Brides is ready to help him find the girl of his dreams. Does it really matter that he lied on his application and really isn't looking for long term, but rather some fast action? Earth women better watch out. Things are about to heat up.

Happy Reading!

MichellePillow.com

ABOUT MICHELLE M. PILLOW

New York Times & *USA TODAY*
Bestselling Author

Michelle loves to travel and try new things, whether it's a paranormal investigation of an old Vaudeville Theatre or climbing Mayan temples in Belize. She believes life is an adventure fueled by copious amounts of coffee.

Newly relocated to the American South, Michelle is involved in various film and documentary projects with her talented director husband. She is mom to a fantastic artist. And she's managed by a dog and cat who make sure she's meeting her deadlines.

For the most part she can be found wearing pajama pants and working in her office. There may or may not be dancing. It's all part of the creative process.

**Come say hello! Michelle loves talking
with readers on social media!**

www.MichellePillow.com

facebook.com/AuthorMichellePillow

twitter.com/michellepillow

instagram.com/michellempillow

bookbub.com/authors/michelle-m-pillow

goodreads.com/Michelle_Pillow

amazon.com/author/michellepillow

youtube.com/michellepillow

pinterest.com/michellepillow

JOIN THE EXCLUSIVE CLUB!

Join the Pillow Fighters' Reader Club to stay informed about new books, sales, contests, giveaways, exclusive content, preorders and more!

michellepillow.com/author-updates

WE THINK YOU'LL LOVE...

Readers who love this series, love the Space Lords!

His Metal Maiden

From NY Times & USA TODAY Bestselling Author, Michelle M. Pillow, a space adventure romance!

Dragon-shifter Lochlann left home to avoid a war he didn't believe in. Now as Captain of The Conqueror, in charge of a misfit crew, all he wants is to return without the label of coward. He's been offered one chance at redemption: Find Margot, a noblewoman's missing sister. The only problem is, the woman disappeared years ago, and his closest lead is a stunningly beautiful look-a-like droid crafted in her image. Alexis is programed to be everything he could ever desire, but getting her to reveal her secrets proves to be a true challenge for this alpha male.

Being a base model pleasure droid isn't as glamorous as it sounds. Alexis can't remember a time when she wasn't the property of others. Multiple surgeries, and endless tests, have amounted to a life not worth living. When a pirate crew visits her facility, she sneaks onto their ship. Desperate not to be returned to her owners, she strikes a deal with the alluring captain. Pretend to be Margot in exchange for freedom.

PLEASE LEAVE A REVIEW
THANK YOU FOR READING!

Please take a moment to share your thoughts by reviewing this book.

Thank you to all the wonderful readers who take the time to share your thoughts about the books you love. I can't begin to tell you how important you are when it comes to helping other readers discover the books!

Be sure to check out Michelle's other titles at www.MichellePillow.com